POKÉMON™
ADVENTURES
GOLD & SILVER

D0013615

Pokémon ADVENTURES

Volume 9

VIZ Kids Edition

Story by **HIDENORI KUSAKA**

Art by **MATO**

© 2010 Pokémon.
© 1995–2010 Nintendo/Creatures Inc./GAME FREAK inc.
TM and ® and character names are trademarks of Nintendo.
© 1997 Hidenori KUSAKA and MATO/Shogakukan
All rights reserved.
Original Japanese edition "POCKET MONSTER SPECIAL"
published by SHOGAKUKAN Inc.

English Adaptation/Gerard Jones
Translation/Kaori Inoue
Touch-up & Lettering/Annaliese Christman
Design/Sam Elzway
Editor/Jann Jones

The rights of the author(s) of the work(s) in this publication to be so identified have been asserted in accordance with the Copyright, Designs and Patents Act 1988. A CIP catalogue record for this book is available from the British Library.

The stories, characters and incidents mentioned in this publication are entirely fictional.

No portion of this book may be reproduced or transmitted in any form or by any means without written permission from the copyright holders.

Printed in the U.S.A.

Published by VIZ Media, LLC
P.O. Box 77010
San Francisco, CA 94107

10 9 8 7 6 5 4
First printing, October 2010
Fourth printing, February 2013

POKÉMON™
ADVENTURES
GOLD & SILVER
9
VOLUME NINE
GYM
Story by
Hidenori Kusaka
Art by Mato

CHARACTERS
THUS FAR...
POKÉMON
Aibo
(Aipom)
Gold, a kid from New Bark Town in the region of Johto, is hot on the trail of Silver, a thief who stole a Totodile from Professor Elm and a Pokédex from Professor Oak…
Joined by Exbo, a Cyndaquil from Elm's lab and a friend of the kidnapped Totodile, Gold catches Silver.
Exbo
(Cyndaquil)
Gold
He can be reckless and relies too much on luck. But his sense of justice when it comes to Pokémon is second to none… and his battle skills get better every day!

MAIN JOURNEY
Silver
A young man of few words. Though there seems to be a reason behind his actions, his mission is a mysterious one. He is a more skilled Trainer than Gold.
Sneasel
Joey
Professor Oak
Gold and Silver finally battle, but then they join against a common foe–Team Rocket, who everyone thinks was destroyed years ago! Once again, Silver slips away. Now Gold really wants to know what he's up to!
Sunbo (Sunkern)
Polibo (Poliwag)
Professor Elm

CONTENTS

SILVER

THIS MUST BE THE GUY WHO JUMPED US...
WHAT DOES HE MEAN, "STAY AWAY FROM THIS FOREST"?

THE ONLY THING I KNOW FOR SURE IS...
HE'S ONE HIGH-LEVEL TRAINER!

SERIOUSLY CREEPY MASK TOO.
I COULD JUST SKIP OUT NOW...

BUT I'D HAVE TO LEAVE THEM BEHIND.
I'VE GOT NO CHOICE...
GG

I'LL NEVER BEAT HIM.
DMM
ALL I CAN DO NOW IS... SAVE MYSELF.

VRR
AND IF YOU BELIEVE THAT—
YOU DON'T KNOW ME VERY WELL!!
TMM
AIBO !!
PULL HIS MASK OFF!
!
104 The Ariados up There
GO, AIBO!
RIP RIP
RIP RIP
A-IEEE!

I GOT 'EM, AIBO!!
NOW LET'S GET OUTTA–

ZSHHH
AGH!

HE-HE-HEH...
SHALL WE GET TO WORK THEN?
WHAT?!
YOU'LL DO WHAT HE DID...
... KEEP INTRUDERS OUT OF THIS FOREST.

SO I WAS RIGHT! YOU USED GASTLY TO CONTROL THIS GUY AND HIS FARFETCH'D!
OF COURSE!

I DON'T KNOW WHAT YOU'RE UP TO HERE— BUT I DON'T LIKE IT!
WHO ARE YOU TO DECIDE WHO COMES INTO THIS FOREST AND WHO DOESN'T ?!

WHAT GIVES YOU THE RIGHT TO TAKE CONTROL OF ANOTHER TRAINER'S POKÉMON?!
NOT TO MENTION TAKING CONTROL OF THEIR BRAIN!!

...
...

BOOM!

YAAAG!

JERK !!

HAK KOF

ZIP

GASTLY—SHADOW BALL!!

TMMM

HOUN-DOUR—IRON TAIL!!

HEY HEY HEY HEY HEY!!

OKAY, EXBO... IT'S ALL ON YOU!

NOD

TOK TOK

CLEVER, USING CYNDAQUIL'S SMOKESCREEN TO BLEND IN TO THE SMOKE FROM THE BLAST.
WHAT?!

HEH
BUT SINCE MY SERVANT IS PROGRAMMED TO FOLLOW HIM...
...AND HE HASN'T REACTED...

FSH...
...THE BOY MUST STILL BE CLOSE.
WHICH MEANS HE MUST BE...
...HIDING IN A TREE!

VLULULU

SHOOT! HE KNOWS!

WHAT NOW?!
I CAN'T BEAT HIM IN A STRAIGHT-UP BATTLE.
PIPI

I JUST WISH I KNEW WHAT HE WAS UP TO...
PIPIPI
WHY'S A GUY WITH THAT KIND OF POWER HIDING IN A FOREST?

DMM
WAGH!!

DMM
USING HEADBUTT TO SHAKE THE TREES—
—AND SPIDER WEB TO CATCH ME!
HOW DO I GET OUT OF THIS?!

SHAKA
SHAKA
EEH.
DMM

SLIP
VSH
YAAA!

KIIII
SSSS
!!
LIGHT... FROM THE SHRINE?!

FOR-GET THE BOY FOR NOW.
KARAKA
WE CAN'T LET THIS CHANCE SLIP AWAY.

YULLU
NOT NOW!
?!
HOLD HIM!
ARIA-DOS!
FSH
HE FELL FOR IT!!
GOT HIM WITH MY TRAP!
WHAT ?!
GIVE 'IM A TASTE OF MEGA DR–

ACK! STRING FROM ITS BUTT TOO?!
FOOL !!
?!
WM
NOW LEAVE HIM!
TING
...
LLLLLLLL
SHOOT ...

SQUIRM
NG... NGHH !!

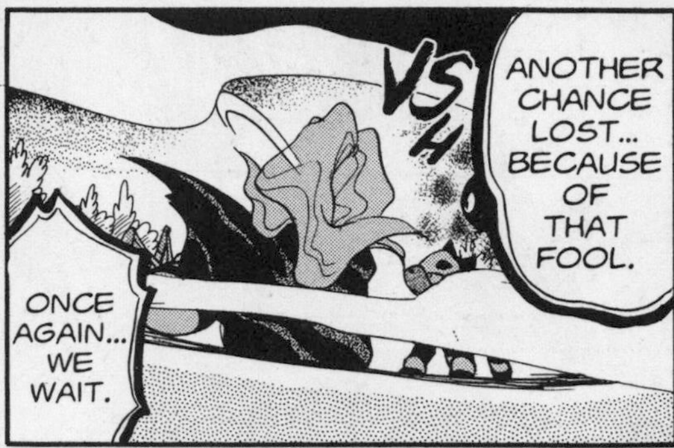
VSHH
ANOTHER CHANCE LOST... BECAUSE OF THAT FOOL.
ONCE AGAIN... WE WAIT.

WHAT'S THE BIG IDEA?!

YOU CAN'T JUST BAIL IN THE MIDDLE OF A BATTLE!
I DEMAND YOU COME BACK!

LOOK...
I DON'T MIND FIGHTING KIDS...

BUT YOU'RE NOT NEARLY AS GOOD AS THAT LAST PUNK I FOUGHT.
THE ONE WITH THE CROCONAW.
OH YEAH ?!

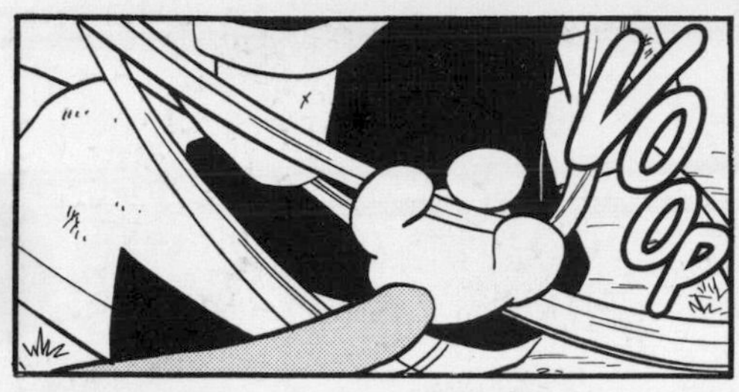
VOOP

ANYWAY, WE'VE GOT TO HURRY UP AND GET THESE GUYS OUT OF THIS CREEPY...

THANKS, AIBO.
THAT CREEP REALLY KNOWS HOW TO PUSH MY BUTTONS.

WHAT'S WITH ALL THE LONG FACES?

GLOOOM
HUH ?

HEY. THIS FIGHT ISN'T OVER.

NOD
NOD
DON'T TELL ME IT'S BECAUSE HE KNOCKED US AROUND?

WE'RE GONNA GET A REMATCH! AND NEXT TIME--
EVERY ONE OF US IS GONNA BE STRONGER!

WE'LL BEAT 'EM NEXT TIME EVEN IF THEY OUTNUMBER US TEN TO ONE!

...

TP

I PROMISE YOU.

ARE YOU ALL RIGHT, GOLD ?!
DEPENDS ON YOUR DEFINITION OF "ALL RIGHT."
HOW ARE THE POKÉMON AND THE TRAINER YOU RESCUED?
ALIVE, BUT BARELY.
PoKé
RIP
RIP
MEANWHILE, I'M ANALYZING THE GOLD POWDER YOU SCANNED AND SENT TO ME.
THAT STUFF WAS ALL OVER AIBO'S TAIL.
I THINK IT WAS UNDER THE GUY'S CAPE.
IT MAY BE IMPORTANT.

GOLD!! ARE YOU LISTEN-ING?!
HUH? OH. YEAH, RIGHT. CARE-FUL.
THE KID WITH THE CROCONAW HE WAS TALKING ABOUT...
...HAS GOT TO BE SILVER. THE TOTODILE MUST HAVE EVOLVED.
THAT GUY'S GOT NERVE SAYING SILVER'S BETTER THAN...

PIRIRIRI
SILVER. NEW DATA.
THE KID CAME INTO CONTACT WITH THE MASKED MAN.
IT WAS IN THE FOREST IN QUES-TION.
AFTERWARD LIGHT WAS SEEN EMANATING FROM THE SHRINE... BUT THE MASKED MAN FAILED TO OBTAIN THE LIGHT.
I WANT YOU TO KEEP UP WITH YOUR SURVEIL-LANCE OF THE MASKED MAN.
I'M ON IT.

VIOLET GYM

VIOLET

VIOLET

RESERVED FOR CEREMONY

CHAK

KRIIIII

TMM

105 Smeargl Smudge

FALKNER, WE NOW DESIGNATE YOU...

...THE NEW LEADER OF VIOLET GYM!!

ALL RIGHT, BILL. WE APPOINTED THIS FALKNER FELLOW AS YOU ASKED. NOW YOU OWE US...
I TOLD YOU! I'M TRYIN' TO FIX THE DANG POKÉMON STORAGE SYSTEM!

BUT IF I CAN'T EVEN FIGURE OUT WHY IT BROKE—
W-WAIT! PLEASE!

I'M HONORED TO HAVE BEEN GIVEN THIS POST.
BUT I'D HATE TO THINK THAT MY APPOINTMENT HAS CAUSED TROUBLE WITHIN THE POKÉMON ASSOCIATION.
IF THERE'S ANYTHING I CAN DO TO HELP...

WELL, WE SURE DO APPRECIATE THAT, SON! BUT NONE O' THIS IS YOUR FAULT!
NONE-THE-LESS ...

WE'LL BE FINE. YOU JUST THINK ABOUT BEIN' A GOOD GYM LEADER. ANOTHER FRIEND O' MINE'S ABOUT TO TAKE THE EXAM TOO...

...AND BETWEEN THE TWO OF YOU... WELL, WE'LL TALK.
RIGHT NOW WE'RE IN THE MIDDLE O' YOUR INSTAL-LATION CERE-MONY!

FALKNER.
FSH
ONE OF THE SACRED RESPONSIBILITIES OF THE GYM LEADER IS TO GUARD THIS...

...THE ZEPHYR BADGE.

TRAINERS WILL SOON BE COMING FROM ALL OVER TO CHALLENGE YOU IN YOUR GYM... YOU MUST TEST THEIR ABILITIES.
YOU ARE TO BESTOW THIS BADGE ONLY ON THOSE WHOM YOU DEEM TRULY WORTHY.

FURTHERMORE...
BLAH BLAH
WELL, GOLD...
I PASSED... USING THE SKARMORY WE CAPTURED TOGETHER.
HOO
YOU WANTED HEAT?!!
I WISH I KNEW HOW TO FIND YOU NOW... OR KNEW HOW YOU'RE DOING, AT LEAST...

GOLDEN-
ROD
CITY
THAT CITY... IS REALLY ...

... HUGE !!

AND ALL THOSE LIGHTS! UP HERE IT'S MIDNIGHT... AND DOWN THERE IT'S AS BRIGHT AS NOON!

IT'S SUPPOSED TO BE FULL OF STORES AND GAME CORNERS AND EVERY-THING!
PIPI

TOO BAD I'VE GOT NO MONEY.
SHKSHK

OH WELL. GUESS WE CAN WORRY ABOUT THAT TOMORROW. G'NIGHT, GANG.
YAWN

SNEAK
ZZZZZ

TP TP TP

ZZZ

SME-HE-HE

FSH
FSH
FSH
FSH

ARRRH!

W... WHA ...?
BLP

I'M SUPPOSED TO GO INTO GOLDEN-ROD CITY LOOKING LIKE THIS?!
WHAT'D YOU DO THAT FOR?!

BING

BOING
NYAA

IT'S HEAD-ING FOR THE CITY !!
RUBRUB

DOMP

YOU GOTTA BE FASTER THAN THAT TO GET AWAY FROM US!

HEEHEE

I CAN'T SEE!! WHERE'D IT GO ?!!
AAAAAGH!
BLAP

SAY. ARE YOU OKAY, KID?
DMM...
THAT STUPID THING TRICKED ME!
NOW WE'LL NEVER CATCH IT!!

LISTEN, KID! YOU HAD A TOUGH OPPONENT, BUT I SAW SOME IMPRESSIVE TEAMWORK AMONGST YOUR POKÉMON!
R-REALLY ?!

I PRODUCE A RADIO SHOW—POKÉMON TALENT ROUND-UP!

I HAPPEN TO BE ON MY WAY TO BROADCAST THE NEXT EPISODE RIGHT NOW. HOW WOULD YOU LIKE TO BE ON IT?!

NOT ONLY AM I GONNA MAKE SOME MONEY...
I CAN'T BELIEVE MY LUCK!!

THIS IS OUR BROAD-CAST HEAD-QUARTERS...

BUT I DO BELIEVE THIS IS THE SAME RADIO STATION WHERE DJ MARY DOES HER SHOW WITH THAT OAK GUY! WHICH MEANS...
...I MIGHT ACTUALLY GET TO MEET HER!!

THE STUDIO IS IN HERE.
I'M THERE!
HUH ?!

BAM
BAM
YOU'RE GONNA BE SORRY YOU EVER PAINTED MY FACE!!
H-HEY!! CUT THAT OUT!!

YOU AGAIN!!

EEEEEE!!
WHAM
BAMBAM
I'M DJ MARY, AND I'LL BE YOUR HOST. MY GUEST TODAY IS WHITNEY, GYM LEADER FOR GOLDENROD... HUH?!
WHAT'S GOING ON OUT...
WHAT DO YOU THINK YOU'RE DOING?!
YOU KNOW THIS GOOF, MARY?!
NEVER SEEN HIM BEFORE.
NO, NO!! IT CAN'T BE!!
THAT FACE-PAINTING PEST CAN'T BELONG TO DJ MARY!

NEW BARK TOWN
MIND IF I PLAY THE RADIO, PROFESSOR? IT'S DJ MARY'S SHOW!
SNAP
NO, IT'S GOTTA BE THIS OTHER CHICK'S!! TELL ME IT'S HERS !!
FOMP

IT S-SOUNDS LIKE HIM... BUT SURELY IT CAN'T...
DRIP

LISTEN, YOU MORON—
MY NAME HAPPENS TO BE GOLD, LADY!
IT CAN.
WMP
SOMEHOW I DON'T THINK HE'S BEING VERY CAREFUL...

BING
ON AIR
OFF AIR
WHAT DO YOU PEOPLE THINK YOU'RE DOING?!

S-SIR!! LISTENERS ARE CALLING IN BY THE HUNDREDS!!
YOU SEE?! COM-PLAINTS !!

ARE YOU TRYING TO DESTROY THIS SHOW?!
I DON'T CARE !!
YOU STARTED IT!
SIGH

ACTUALLY... MOST OF THEM WERE ALONG THE LINES OF "THIS LINEUP IS HOT" AND "WHY DON'T YOU LET THEM BATTLE FOR REAL?"
FOMP
WELL, IF THAT'S WHAT THEY WANT...
I'M MORE THAN HAPPY TO GIVE IT TO THEM.

STOP IT, BOTH OF YOU!!
SIR! HOW DO WE MAKE THEM STOP THIS?!
HMM ...

I GAVE SMEA-SMEA TO DJ MARY. IF YOU HAVE A PROBLEM WITH THAT... WE'LL SETTLE IT ON THE AIR!!
HEY, THE BIGGER THE STAGE, THE BETTER I FIGHT !!

I THINK WHAT THIS NEEDS IS A TWO-HOUR SPECIAL!!
FOMP

POP
POP
SHOO
SHOO

YOU DE-MANDED IT... YOU'VE GOT IT!
GOLD THE MYSTERY BOY VS. OUR LOCAL GYM LEADER... WHITNEY!!
I CAN'T BELIEVE THIS...

THEY'LL FOLLOW **POKÉMON BATTLE RACE** RULES—FROM GOLDENROD CITY THROUGH THE NATIONAL PARK TO THE GOAL—THE ROUTE 37 ROAD SIGN!!
AND OF COURSE—BATTLING ALL THE WAY!!

THIS PROGRAM IS BROUGHT TO YOU BY **THE BIKE SHOP** TO CELEBRATE THEIR NEW GOLDENROD CITY HEAD-QUARTERS!
WE'LL PROVIDE COMPLETE LIVE COVERAGE THROUGH OUR MOBILE BROADCAST-ING VANS!

BUT WHY DO I HAVE TO RIDE A BIKE ?!
I'LL FIGHT ANY-BODY !!
IT'S NOT FAIR !!
I SHOULD BE PUSHING A BOARD, NOT PEDALS!
OKAY. I'M READY WHEN YOU ARE.
AND I'M BORROWING SMEA-SMEA-RIGHT, MARY?
THIS IS SMEA-SMEA'S FIGHT TOO!
MIRACLE

SORRY. OUR SPONSOR MAKES BIKES.
AND THEY WANT TO HEAR US TALK ABOUT THEIR PRODUCT!
MIRACLE
THEIR LOGO ...
!!

WHOA WHOA!! WHAT ARE YOU DOING?!
ZIP
ZIP
ZIP
ZIP
THEN HOW 'BOUT THIS?!

... MY OWN WHEELS !!
IT'S STILL GOT TWO WHEELS, RIGHT?

MIRACLE

SO LET'S GET THIS GOING !!
WELL... I GUESS THAT COUNTS ...

OKAY... ON YOUR MARKS... GET SET...
MIRACLE
MIRACLE

GO!!

WRRRL

MILMIL!! ROLL-OUT!!

GONK

TM

THERE'S AN ODD **TREE** IN THE MIDDLE OF THE ROAD!!

AND I **SWEAR** IT WASN'T HERE YESTERDAY !!

HAS THAT LINE EVER ACTUALLY WORKED FOR YOU?!

WAIT !!!

106 How Do You Do, Sudowoodo?

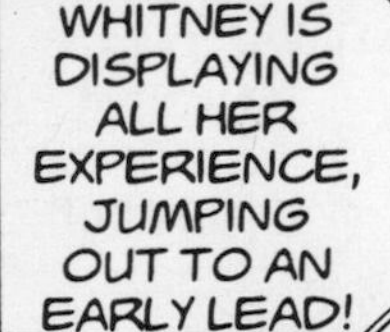

THE POKÉMON BATTLE RACE IS UNDER WAY!!

AND SHE'S GOT TWO POKÉMON— SMEARGLE AND MILTANK—

THEY'RE ABOUT TO ENTER... WHAT?!
WHAT'S THE BIG IDEA?!
WHO PUT THAT STUPID TREE THERE ?!
SKRIIII

I HAD THIS RACE WON!!
WHOSE FAULT IS THIS?!
NOT MINE, NOT MINE!

?!!
WHAT THE-?!
SSSH
SKCH
YOU SEE?! HE CAUGHT UP!!
IS THAT A TREE?!

DM
ROLL-OUT!!
I'LL JUST HAVE TO TAKE CARE OF IT MY-SELF!!
WRRRR
I'M SUR-ROUND-ED BY IDIOTS!!

W-W-WHAT KIND OF TREE IS THIS?!

THUD

FOOM
EXBO-EMBER!!

I'LL SHOW YOU HOW IT'S DONE!!
ZM

LIKE YOU SAID...
W-W-WHAT KIND OF TREE IS THIS?!
FWOOSH
HOW AM I SUPPOSED TO WIN WITH THAT THING IN THE WAY?!
THAT'S MY LINE!!
TIME TO GO ALL OUT! AIBO! SUNBO! POLIBO!
WAK
WAK
SPYU
BR R BRR
WEIRD.
THE ONLY THING IT REACTED TO WAS POLIBO'S WATER ATTACK...
!!
TMM TMM TMM
ARE THOSE... FOOT-STEPS?!!
NOW WHAT?!

EEEYAAA!!!

TOOM

FIRST AN INDESTRUC-TIBLE TREE BLOCKING THE ROUTE ...
NOW A WILD POKÉ-MON!!

VIP VIP

IS IT LOOKING FOR SOME-THING?
DON'T JUST STAND THERE, IDIOT!! THAT'S RHYDON !!

IT'LL CRUSH YOU WITHOUT BATTING AN EYE!!
WE HAVE TO STRIKE FIRST!!
VSH

WOOM

GLARE
GASP

MILMIL
!!
GGGG

!
WK

...!!
TOOM
TOOM
OUR GYM LEADER'S BEEN KIDNAPPED BY A WILD RHYDON!!

WHIT-
NEY!!

KOFF!
BOOR

SAVE HER!!
THE RACE IS OFF!! ALL VANS— GET RHYDON !!
BRRROOM

WHERE DO YOU THINK YOU'RE GOIN' WITHOUT...
HUH ?!

IT'S SHAKING AGAIN... SAME AS BEFORE!

BRRR
BRRR
BRR

HEY!! POLIBO !!
DO THAT SAME WATER GUN AGAIN!!
SSSH
SPYUU

WAIT A MINUTE... YOU MEAN...

YOU'RE A POKÉ-MON ?!!

!

VOOP VOOP

VOOP VOOP

NOD

THAT CRAZY RHYDON— ARE YOU WHAT IT WAS AFTER ?!

NOD

Sudowoudo
Imitation Pokémon
Height 3' 11''
Weight 83.8 lbs
No. 185
Disguises as tree to avoid being attacked. Dislikes water, includin
rain.
Cry Area

MAN, THAT WAS THE BEST TREE IMITATION I'VE EVER SEEN!

BUT WHAT'S THE BIG IDEA ?!

YOU HIDING FROM SOME-TH...

OH!!

GEEZ. NOW I FEEL BAD.
WAK
WAK
I MEAN, IF WE'D JUST LEFT YOU ALONE AND WAITED...
WE COULDA SAVED YOU A LOT OF STRESS!

SO WHAT HAPPENS WHEN THAT RHYDON COMES AFTER YOU AGAIN?

SOONER OR LATER YOU'RE GONNA HAVE TO STAND UP TO IT!

BRR
BRR

WHAT ARE YOU AFRAID OF?! YOU BRUSHED OFF ALL OUR ATTACKS!
YOU'RE A TOTAL HERO!!

OKAY.
!!
I GUESS I'M GONNA HAVE TO SAVE YOU FROM YOURSELF!
YOU'RE GONNA LEARN—

—HOW TO FIGHT!!
VSH

NOW GET THIS THROUGH YOUR HEAD. YOU'RE STRONG ENOUGH TO BRUSH OFF MILTANK'S BEST ATTACK. YOU'VE GOT NOTHING TO FEAR!
NOD

THERE !!

I'M GONNA SHOOT YOUR POKÉ BALL AS CLOSE TO IT AS I CAN. THE INSTANT YOU HIT THE GROUND, POP OUT–

–AND HIT RHYDON BEFORE IT REALIZES IT'S YOU!!
KLAK

YOU CAN ONLY DO THIS ONCE, SO–
HOOO

CHK

DO IT!!
VOOP

WAM

STUDIO
THE RACE MAY BE CANCELED, BUT THE WINNER'S CLEAR!

NEH HEH HEH HEH HEH!!

I MEAN, WHO MOVED THE IMMOVABLE TREE, HUH?
AND WHO HAD TO RESCUE HIS OPPONENT?! WAHAHA!
You got lucky!

SPCH
HEY!

I GUESS I DESERVE A LITTLE RESPECT, EH, SMEARGLE?
HONK

NEXT TIME, PUNK... WE'RE GONNA HAVE A REAL MATCH!!

WHY, YOU CHEESY LITTLE—
UM, GOLD? HOW MANY AUTOGRAPHS DID YOU SAY?
WAM WOOD

HUH ?!
DM DM DM

NOW THAT I'VE GOT SOME CASH, I'M GOING TO THE GAME CORNER!
O-KAY !!

YOU WANT TO COME WITH US, HUH? WELL, OKAY... SUDOBO!

...

GLEAM

SHP

TK
KLAK
107
Gligar Glide

KONK

KONK

WHOA!
THAT KID'S INCRED-IBLE!!

AWW ...
IT'S NOTHIN'!

TOMP
SHULULU
LOOK AT THAT!!
SKRIK
HOW DOES A BALL CURVE LIKE THAT?! IT'S UNREAL!!
KWRRR

?!
IN FACT... ISN'T IT A LITTLE TOO UNREAL?!

PLIP PLIP
RRRIP
OH... NO!

ALL THOSE MOVES—WERE FROM THAT THING?!
YOU DISGUISED A POKÉ BALL AS A POOL BALL?!
Heh heh. Clever, huh?!

FOMP
PLIP

FYOOOOOO
GAME
GET OUTTA HERE!!

A CALL ON MY POKÉ-GEAR! MAYBE IT'S THAT PICNICKER GIRL!
She totally dug me.
PIP
PRRRRRT

HMPH.
SOME PEOPLE CAN'T TAKE A JOKE.

WELL, GOLD.
▶Professor Elm
!!
I HEARD YOU ON THE RADIO THE OTHER DAY.
HAVING FUN?!
YEEPS! PRO-FESSOR ?!

WHAT'S THE STATUS OF YOUR POKÉMON TEAM AT PRESENT ?
EXBO... THAT'S YOUR CYNDA-QUIL... IS DOING GREAT!
SO ARE AIBO THE AIPOM, POLIBO THE POLI-WAG...
...SUNBO THE SUNKERN... AND A NEW ONE...
...SUDOBO THE SUDO-WOODO.
OH, AND THE EGG!!
IT'S... WELL... STILL AN EGG!
▶Exbo
Aibo
Egg

GOOD. THE EGG IS WHY I'M CALLING. EVEN I DON'T KNOW WHAT KINDS OF CHANGES IT MAY GO THROUGH.
PROMISE ME YOU'LL KEEP A VERY CLOSE EYE ON IT!
CLICK. BEEP BEEP BEEP.
GEEZ. BOSSY, BOSSY!

AN EGG, HUH ...?

HOOT
HOOT

YAWW
WISH I KNEW WHAT POKÉMON IT WAS FROM.

TNK

MAYBE SOMETHING REALLY STRONG...
ONE THAT CAN BEAT ANY POKÉMON WITH ONE PUNCH...
YEAH, RIGHT. HEH HEH...
ZZZ ZZZ.

ROLL
!

TWAP

SHNORR
FOMP
NOT HUNGRY ...

SHAKA
SHAKA
NNN... NO...

WIIIN

SLIP

BOING

Gligar
FlyScorpion
Pokemon
Height
Weight
No. 207

THUK

PLIP
BLOOOSH
TP
SHOOO
NNNNN...

NWUK!
WHEEE!
DM
FOOSH

SIZZLE
GNAAA

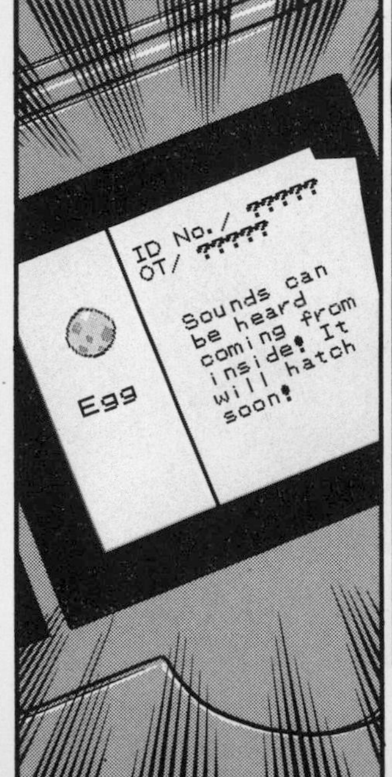
ID No./ ?????
OT/ ?????
Sounds can be heard coming from inside! It will hatch soon!
Egg

KRIK
BRR
BRRR
KRIIK...
BRRR
BRR
KRIIIII
KRIK

KRAAK

HYAH!

GUUUH
MMMM?
WMP
FOOO
WHUD
NOP

TK TK TK TK TK

HWEEEEN

HYAH!

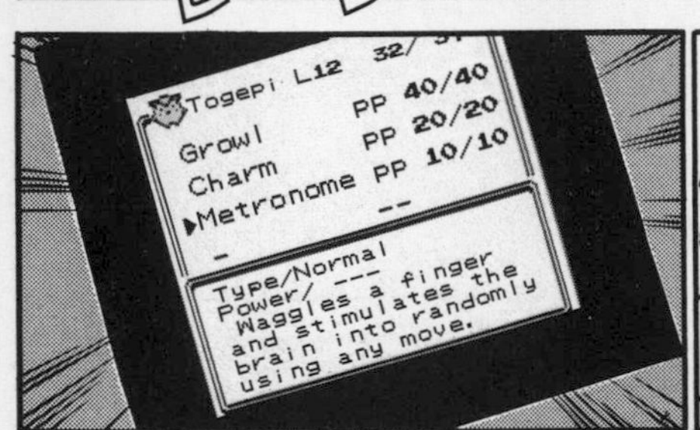

WOA
GYOOOO
BONK
FWCH
?!
VIP

HA HA HA
NOTHING?! RAISING THE EGG'S LEVEL UNTIL IT HATCHED ?!
MAY AS WELL TAKE CREDIT.

AW, IT WAS NOTHING!! SERIOUSLY... NOTHING!!
GOLDEN-ROD CITY POKÉ-MON CENTER
PC

SO SHOW ME WHAT THIS NEWLY HATCHED POKÉMON CAN DO!!
SURE THING !!

SHAKE SHAKE
TNK TNK TNK
HUH ?

WSH
TNK

SHUFFLE!
VIP

YOU'VE TURNED THIS POKÉMON INTO A...A...A DELINQUENT !!

AS IF IT'S NOT BAD ENOUGH BEING YELLED AT...

NOW I'VE GOTTA GO THROUGH THIS TOO.

SHF
SHF
HUH
?

POINT
WAGH!

JUST TOO BAD WE GOTTA BACK-TRACK... SOUTH OF GOLDEN-ROD, HE SAID...

POING

POING

WHO **ARE** ALL THESE LITTLE ONES?!

THIS MUST BE THE POKÉMON DAY CARE!
AND AN OLD LADY ?!
SHF
OHHH, WAIT! WAIT! WAIT!

WHAT ELSE ARE YOU?!
...DARE YOU CALL ME AN OLD LADY, YOU YOUNG RUFFIAN?!

HOW ...
GLARE

AWP.
SHOVE
TO MAKE UP FOR YOUR RUDENESS, HELP ME CATCH THEM!
AND HURRY !!

WHEW.

GOOD THING FOR US, EH, SWEETIE?
IF THIS LAD HADN'T COME AROUND, WE'D'VE LOST THEM ALL!

THE FENCE BROKE DOWN, AND THEY WERE RUNNING ALL OVER. WE'RE GLAD YOU WERE PASSING BY!
THOSE THINGS ARE... HUFF... HUFF... FAST!

PRO-FESSOR ELM TOLD US YOU'D BE COMING.
OH, ARE YOU THAT GOLD BOY? WELL, WE'RE THE DAY CARE COUPLE YOU'RE LOOKING FOR!

I HEAR YOU HATCHED THAT EGG WE FOUND, EH?
GOOD JOB!

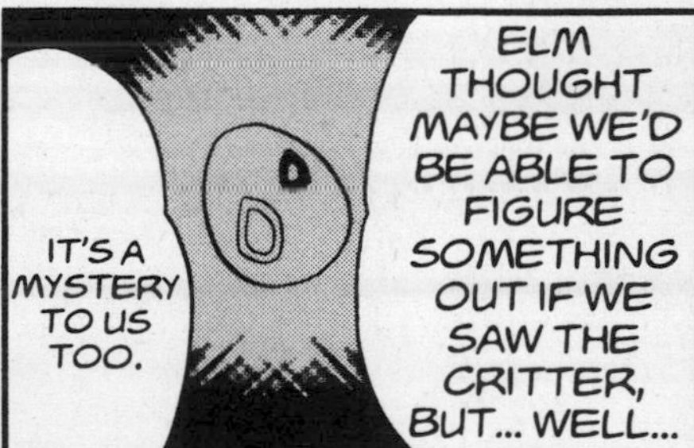
ELM THOUGHT MAYBE WE'D BE ABLE TO FIGURE SOMETHING OUT IF WE SAW THE CRITTER, BUT... WELL...
IT'S A MYSTERY TO US TOO.

WE WERE TAKING CARE OF TWO POKÉMON... DON'T EVEN KNOW WHAT THEY WERE.
WHAT ?!!
SUDDENLY THEY WERE GONE... AND THERE WAS AN EGG!

GEEZ... SO NOTHING TO REPORT TO ELM... AGAIN.

WE KEEP WATCHING TO SEE IF ANYONE ELSE LAYS ONE, BUT NO LUCK.

WELL, GUESS I'LL BE GOING!
CIAO!
WAIT !!!

YOU'RE AT THE FAMOUS POKÉMON DAY CARE!

NO BETTER PLACE FOR TIPS ON RAIS-ING THEM RIGHT!

YOU COULD MAKE THOSE POKÉMON OF YOURS MIGHTY STRONG!
REALLY ?!

YOU DON'T HAVE TO ASK ME TWICE!!
I DIDN'T THINK SO.

THIS IS MY CHANCE TO SHRINK THE GAP BETWEEN ME AND SILVER-FAST!!
I'M NOT GETTING ANY YOUNGER. I NEED ALL THE HELP I CAN GET TO KEEP UP WITH THESE ZANIES!

SO... ANOTHER ONE CAUGHT IN GRANDMA'S WEB, EH?
AH, WELL.
MAYBE I'D BETTER GIVE HER A CALL...
TNK

PRRRT ...
CHK
HELLO ?
IT'S ME, THE OLD FELLER... FROM THE DAY CARE.
REMEMBER THAT MYSTERIOUS EGG WE FOUND? WELL, IT HATCHED.
I'M LOOKING AT THE LITTLE CRITTER RIGHT NOW.
WANT TO SEE IT?
ARE YOU KIDDING ?!
COME ANYTIME, JASMINE.
COOL, I'M ON MY WAY NOW!!

C'MON, C'MON! PICK UP YOUR FEET!
WHERE ARE WE GOING ?
BACK DOOR OF THE BREED-ING CENTER.
HUH ?

WOW! THAT'S A LOT OF BOOKS!
GRANDPA'S RESEARCH LIBRARY.

"POKÉMON LEAGUE PAST WINNERS" ?
FLIP

POLI-WRATH, HUH...
WINNER RED
WHOA!

POLIBO, ARE YOU GONNA LOOK LIKE THIS WHEN YOU GROW UP?!
WHEE WHEE
TAKE GOOD CARE OF POLIBO AND IT WILL!
KRIII

HERE WE ARE. GO ON IN.
KTNKKTNK
KIND OF DARK, ISN'T IT...?
?
KLANG!
HUH?
YOU HAVE TO BEAT THEM ALL IN BATTLE BY THE END OF THE DAY. AND I WON'T LET YOU OUT UNTIL YOU DO!
WHAT ?!
108
Quilava Quandary

THEY'RE OUR ELITE FIGHTERS. PERFECT FOR TOUGHENING YOU UP. SO START!
WHO ARE THESE POKÉ-MON?!
TAK
BUT I'LL SHOW YOU!!
NOT EXACTLY WHAT I HAD IN MIND...

DOOM
UM... OF COURSE NOT.
YOU'RE NOT TELLING ME YOU CAN'T FIGHT WITHOUT THOSE GIMMICKS?
FINE THEN.
OKAY, I GOT IT! POWERS AND KNOWL-EDGE!
BLAH BLAH
YOU SHOULDN'T RELY ON ANYTHING BUT THEIR POWERS AND YOUR KNOWL-EDGE!
THIS IS POKÉ-MON TRAIN-ING!
LET'S GET IN THE ZONE...
VSH
... AND GO!!
I DON'T THINK THIS'LL BE FINISHED TODAY.
OH DEAR.

THESE POKÉMON ARE ALL VETERAN FIGHTERS!

YEEE!

WAP

WOM

ACK!

ROLLLL
PFF
AGH! IT'S NOT WORKING!!
FWOOSH
WE'VE JUST GOTTA FIGHT BACK!
EXBO! EMBER!
THAT'S A GROUND-TYPE! BRING YOUR FIRE-TYPE BACK AND USE A WATER-TYPE!
HUH?! O-OKAY! EXBO, BACK!!
IF THEY TRY TO MOVE IN CLOSE, HIT 'EM WITH A LONG-RANGE ATTACK BEFORE THEY'RE IN POSITION!
NOW... HIT 'EM WITH WATER GUN!!
PSHUUU
WHOA! IT WORKED!!
STRENGTH DOESN'T MATTER IF YOUR TIMING'S RIGHT.
HMPH
ARE YOU FIGURING OUT HOW TO DO THIS?

ECRU-TEAK CITY
SIGH
I WISH OLIVINE AND ECRU-TEAK WEREN'T SO FAR APART.

I WONDER WHAT KIND OF POKÉMON CAME OUT OF THAT EGG?
GIGGLE
I CAN'T WAIT TO SEE IT!

DMM
!
WHAT ?!
EARTH-QUAKE ?!

OH ...
KRKK
YAAAA!
KRAAAK

I DON'T HAVE ANYBODY STRONG AGAINST FIGHTING-TYPES...
RRG...
SUDO-BO-MIMIC !!
WAP
HERE IT COMES!! PRIMEAPE'S CROSS CHOP!!
I KNOW !!
AND NONE OF THIS SMOKE-SCREEN NON-SENSE!
I KNOW !!
REMEM-BER... SLOW AND STEADY !!
PI PI
YES! AN ATTACK THAT BOOSTS FIRE ATTACKS!
PI PI
IF THERE WAS SOME WAY TO BOOST OUR POWER...
FOOF!
NOW, EXBO-EMBER !!
GLEEEM
SUNBO! SUNNY DAY!!

WHOOSH
I GUESS THAT'S WHAT OAK SAW IN HIM WHEN HE GAVE HIM THE POKÉDEX.
HOW IS IT GOING, SWEET-IE?
COULD BE WORSE. BOY'S GOT POTEN-TIAL.
GRIN

!
BOOM
LOOKS LIKE IT EVOLVED INTO QUILAVA.
NOW, ARE YOU GONNA LISTEN TO ME OR NOT?
GRAND-MA... I'LL FOLLOW YOU TO THE ENDS OF THE EARTH!!
YOU DO THAT.
FOMP
NOW, LET'S TAKE CARE OF THE REST!!
VN VN
THAT'S THE TICKET!
OH WELL ...

HMM...
OH!
YOU'RE RIGHT!
WE HAVE SOMEONE HERE WHO CAN HELP!
PHEW!

MAN ...
TNK
ECRU-TEAK CITY
THIS IS REALLY BAD.
I JUST HOPE I CAN FIND THIS GIRL IN THE MIDST OF ALL THIS...
WE NEED YOU TO SEARCH FOR HER.
HER NAME IS JAS-MINE.
BUT WHY ME?
YOU'RE RIGHT. IT'S PROBABLY MORE THAN YOU CAN HANDLE.
HMF
OH YEAH ?!
I'LL SHOW YOU WHAT I CAN HANDLE !!
HA HA HA!
THAT'S THE SPIRIT!

I'D LIKE TO TELL YOU THAT YOU'VE MASTERED YOUR TRAINING.
BUT HONESTLY, THESE ARE JUST THE BASICS. FROM HERE ON OUT...

...YOU'LL HAVE TO HONE YOUR SKILLS ON YOUR OWN.
HERE.
A REWARD FOR YOUR HARD WORK.

THE KING'S ROCK.
IT MAY COME IN HANDY.

RRM
!
AFTER-SHOCKS!

WE GOTTA HURRY!!
NOD

COME ON, EXBO!
VSH

FWUP
TAK
...
THE EARTH'S BEEN... COM-PLETELY SHAT-TERED.
VSSH
LET'S GO!

HUH...? THAT LIGHT FROM THE TOWER...

GLEEM

GLEEM

109 Ampharos Amore

KRIIII...

MORE AFTER-SHOCKS !!

WAAGH !!

RKRKK

THE TOWER LOOKS LIKE IT'S...

... ABOUT TO GO DOWN!!

NH...

RRRM

WHO... ARE YOU...?

SHMP

GLEEM
HEY! I SEE IT!!

!

SILVER?! WHAT ARE YOU DOING HERE?!

WHAT ARE YOU GONNA DO WITH HER?!
I HAP-PENED TO FIND HER... AND THOUGHT I'D HELP.

TSK
YOU AGAIN ...

WMP
YOU EXPECT ME TO BELIEVE YOU'D HELP ANOTHER ...
HEY!
FINE. THEN YOU TAKE HER.

WHA ...?
VR

PI PI

?
WHAT'S HE UP TO...?

A SCULP-TURE OF A POKÉ-MON?!

"HO-OH," HUH...?

HO-OH

KREEEEE
THAT SOUNDS...
UH-OH.
RRRRM...
WHOA! CAN'T STAND AROUND HERE!
KOOM
GYAAAAA!
GOTTA GET OUT!
THE TOWER'S COMIN' APART!
RAK RAK RAK RAK
SILVER'S URSARING!

KOOM
THE EXIT ...!!
DON'T JUST STAND THERE! GET HER OUT!
OKAY, OKAY!
CARRY HER OUT!
SHM
SHE MADE IT!
NNG
BOM
BUT NOW... WE'RE TRAP-PED!
PAF
...
KOOM
YAGH !!

K
K
KRIII...
THERE'S GOTTA BE ANOTHER WAY OUT!
WE'RE JUST GONNA HAVE TO FIND IT FAST, THAT'S ALL!
IT'S SINKING EVEN FASTER THAN I THOUGHT ...

WISH IT WASN'T SO DARK...
BRRR

OH! EXBO! LIGHT!!
FSH
!!

IDIOT!!
WE'RE IN A SEALED SPACE!!
FIRE WILL EAT UP ALL OUR OXYGEN!!
WHY DO YOU KEEP GETTING IN MY WAY?!
I JUST CAME TO RESCUE THE GIRL!
I DIDN'T WANT TO SEE YOU!

!!
K
K
R
R
K
N-NOW WHAT?!
K
K

KA-BOOOM
THE WALLS !!
LAND-SLIDE! WE'LL BE CRUSHED!
NO !!
HOOOM
EXBO! BLAST THROUGH THE CEILING!!
SKWISH
NO LUCK!
WMMM
OH GREAT ...
SILVER, DO SOME-THING!!
!
ICE ?!
GET OUT YOUR WATER-TYPE POKÉ-MON!!
WHAT GOOD IS WATER GONNA DO AT A TIME LIKE THIS?!
WMM...

...ARE TIED TO THE POWERS OF NATURE! SO...
RIGHT! POKÉ-MON POWERS ...
IT CAN PULL UP UNDER-GROUND WATER— AND WE'LL USE THAT FORCE TO ESCAPE!
CHK
BOM
BOM
CROCO-NAW!
POLIBO !!

SPHUU
ALL THE WATER YOU CAN!!
...

WHAT'S WRONG WITH YOU?
YOU MAY AS WELL USE A SQUIRT GUN!

WE NEED A SOURCE OF REAL POWER! WE...
HUH ?

BRRR
BRRR

WOOHOO! HE EVOLVED !!

SKWEEZ

BOMF

WHATEVER YOU'RE PLANNING...

...HAD BETTER BE... AGH!

DMM

KAOOMMMM

MMMM...

POLIBO EVOLVED AGAIN ?!
WHIRL-POOL!!
BOOSH
BUT... IT'S NOT POLI-WRATH ?!
WHAT ?!
FOR WATER POWER, POLITOED IS BEST.
IT'S A TRADE EVO-LUTION.
THIS POKÉMON HAS TWO FINAL FORMS.
WD
WHAT DID YOU JUST DO?!
TM
OWW!

WH- WHO IN THE...?

DOOM...

!

SO WHAT ARE THESE KIDS DOING IN THE TIN TOWER?

TEAM ROCKET ?!

110 Piloswine Whine

TM
TM
ASSUME BATTLE POSITIONS!
!
BM BM BM BM BM
AGH!
BM BM ... BM
HEY, SILVER !!
WE'RE SITTING TARGETS OUT HERE!!
STUPID.
HEY!
BOOM

THERE'S GOTTA BE THIRTY OF 'EM!
WHAT ARE THEY GONNA DO WITH A FORCE LIKE THIS?

!!
THEY'VE ALREADY DONE IT.

THE DESTRUCTION OF ECRUTEAK...
...WAS A GIFT FROM THESE TEAM ROCKET THUGS.

WHAT?!

SO YOU KNOW THAT TOO, EH?
WHO ARE YOU?

WAIT...

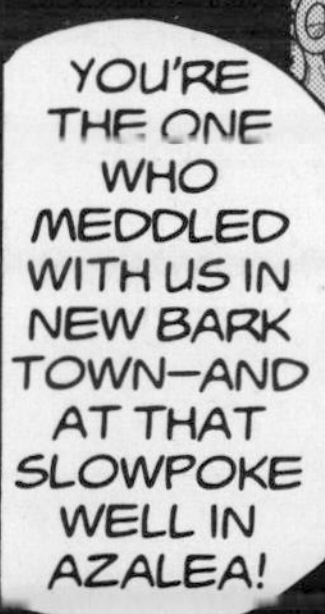
I'VE HEARD ABOUT A KID WITH RED HAIR...
YOU'RE THE ONE WHO MEDDLED WITH US IN NEW BARK TOWN—AND AT THAT SLOWPOKE WELL IN AZALEA!

VSH
DOM
DON'T UNDER-ESTIMATE THIS PUNK!
TAKE HIM OUT—NOW!!

WK
WK
WK
?!

Y'KNOW, I THOUGHT SOMEBODY MIGHT'VE INTERFERED IN MY BATTLE WITH SILVER BACK IN NEW BARK TOWN!
SO IT WAS YOU GUYS!

EVEN MORE REASON NOT TO LIKE YOU! LET'S TAKE 'EM, SILVER!!

WILL YOU JUST STAY OUT OF MY FIGHTS?

THIS IS MY FIGHT!!

R RR...
SNEER
OR MAYBE YOU'RE FORGET-TING WHAT WE CAN DO?

SNAP
WE'LL JUST DESTROY YOU BOTH...
... AT THE SAME TIME.

RRMMMMBL
AN-OTHER QUAKE!
OH MAN...

KOOM
WHOA!
KOOM
IT'S HERE! WHATEVER CAUSED THE EARTH MOVE-MENT!

LOOK OUT!!
TM TM TM
KRRK

BWOOM

IT'S... HUGE !!

YOU'RE SAYING THIS THING CAUSED THE EARTHQUAKE?!
I AM.
ICE AND GROUND... TWO TYPES UNITED IN THE PILOSWINE.
BUT EVEN I DIDN'T REALIZE HOW BIG THE THINGS CAN GET.

GREAT!
CHK
BUT WE CAN'T JUST KEEP RUNNING!

POLIBO! WATER GUN!!
...
HOP HOP
HUH ...?
W-WHAT'S THE MATTER, POLIBO?!

WRA HAHA HA!
TMM
THIS KID'S EVEN LAMER THAN THE RED-HEAD!
I'LL LEAVE THESE GUYS TO YOU.
YOU'LL WHAT?!
VSH

TAKE DOWN!! ROCK SMASH!!
IT HAS THE POWER TO SHATTER THE EARTH UNDER A WHOLE CITY!!
AND IT'S GOING TO KEEP CRUSHING THE GROUND— UNTIL YOU'VE GOT NOWHERE TO STAND! THEN WE'LL SEE HOW LONG YOUR POKÉMON CAN CARRY YOU!

...
THINK SO?
BUT YOU KNOW WHAT HAP-PENS, DON'T YOU...
...WHEN THE GROUND GETS SHAKEN BADLY ENOUGH?

IT'S CALLED... LIQUE-FACTION!

VWSH
WHIRL-
POOL
!!
H-
HEY
!!
NO
WAY
!!
TM
WHEN
SHOCK
WAVES
MAKE
SOLIDS
...
...
BEHAVE
LIKE
LIQUIDS!
ALL
FORCES!
DMDMDM
LEAVE
THE OTHER
KID! WE'VE
GOT TO...

SNEER

HEY, SILVER SAID HE WAS LEAVING 'EM TO ME.

W- WHAT ?!

SORRY. I KINDA BEAT 'EM ALL.

!!

WE'VE ATTACKED THE TIN TOWER AS PLANNED.
NO. WE CAN'T GET IN ANY DEEPER.
IF WE'RE RIGHT ABOUT THE INSTINCTS OF HO-OH... THEN OUR MISSION HAS ALREADY BEEN COM-PLETED.
!

HO-OH ?!

VSH
ALL FORCES... RETREAT !!
RRRGH.

I'M GETTIN' SICK OF THIS!
HEY, WAIT !!
TM
TM
TM
TM

WHY WOULD TEAM ROCKET ATTACK ECRU-TEAK CITY?

NO WONDER IT WOULDN'T LISTEN TO ME...
THAT WAS A LOAN, NOT A GIFT.
GIVE ME BACK MY POLI-BO.

HEY.
VP

I GUESS THAT DAY CARE TRAINING WAS WORTH IT!
PSSSH
HEHEH! YOU COULD TELL, HUH?

LOOKS LIKE YOU'VE GOTTEN BETTER.
...
PIP

WEL-COME BACK, POLIBO!
WHEW
HOP

BOOM

BY THE WAY, SILVER.
PING
WHO'S "HO-OH"?

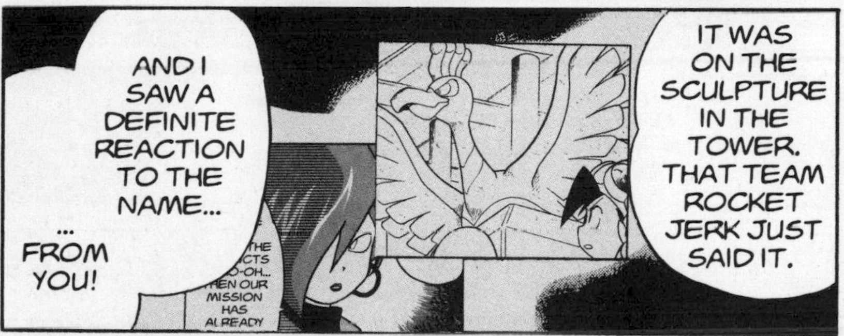
IT WAS ON THE SCULPTURE IN THE TOWER. THAT TEAM ROCKET JERK JUST SAID IT.
THEN OUR MISSION HAS ALREADY
AND I SAW A DEFINITE REACTION TO THE NAME...
... FROM YOU!

WHAT'S THIS ALL ABOUT?
...

YOU CAME HERE FOR A REASON. I KNOW IT.
HMF
WELL, I DON'T NEED TO KNOW THAT.

BUT AT LEAST ANSWER ME THIS.
TM

WHENEVER YOU BATTLE, IT SEEMS LIKE IT'S JUST...
...TO ACCOMPLISH SOMETHING, PART OF SOME PLAN.

HAVE YOU EVER REALLY **ENJOYED** A POKÉMON BATTLE?
WHAT?

YOU HEARD ME.
CHK

WE'VE BOTH GOT A POKÉDEX AND A POKÉMON FROM PROFESSOR ELM.
THAT'S ABOUT AS FAIR A PLAYING FIELD AS YOU'RE EVER GONNA FIND.
WHAT DO YOU SAY?

NNH...

WHERE AM I...?
DON'T WORRY. YOU'RE AT THE EVAC-UATION SHELTER.

AMPHY ...
SIGH
THIS MEANS PEOPLE ARE STILL ALIVE OUT THERE!
WE'LL WAIT FOR DAYLIGHT AND SEND OUT A RESCUE PARTY.

VOOP
WHAT ABOUT THE PEOPLE WHO RESCUED ME FROM INSIDE THE TOWER...?
N-NO! YOU SHOULDN'T GET UP YET!
THE PEOPLE WHO SAVED YOU...? THIS AMPHAROS IS THE ONE WHO CARRIED YOU HERE.
THEN... WAS IT A DREAM ...?

NO. IT'S HAZY... BUT I DO REMEMBER.
TWO YOUNG GUYS WHO RISKED THEIR LIVES TO RESCUE ME FROM THE CRUMBLING TOWER...

UM... WHAT ABOUT THE AREA AROUND THE TIN TOWER ...?
IT'S BEEN CLOSED OFF UNTIL MORNING. NO ONE SHOULD BE THERE NOW.
OH... I SEE...
THIS LOOKS GOOD.

ALREADY TOTALLY DESTROYED ANYWAY.

OKAY THEN.
POP
POP
POP
POP

LET'S USE SIX POKÉ- MON EACH.
WE CAN DO TAG TEAM MODE.
ROLL
ROLL

WEEEN
WE'RE IN LUCK!
THE EMERGENCY POWER IS STILL WORKING! FIRST, WE BETTER HEAL OUR POKÉ- MON...

HUH? HOW COME YOU'VE ONLY GOT FIVE?
VNN
I'M GIVING YOU A ONE- POKÉ- MON HANDI- CAP.

ALTHOUGH I COULD PROBABLY GIVE YOU FOUR AND STILL WIN.
CHK
GRRR
YOU TALK BIG.

CHK
WELL, IT'S TIME TO STOP TALKING...

...AND FIGHT !!

BOOM

111 Tyranitar War

PSSSH

WATER GUN!

EMBER !!

SHOOT!

I'M ALREADY IN A HOLE!

MMF

DOUBLE TEAM!
GOMP
BITE !!
PF
BETTER PACE YOUR-SELF!!
THIS ISN'T ENDING THAT FAST!
TINK
MWK
POP !!
BOM
SHOOT!
IT GREW NEW TEETH ?!
VNN
EXBO !!
KOMP

GLEEEEM
SUNBO! HELP EXBO!!
SUNNY DAY!
PING
BOM
I DON'T THINK SO. BLIZZARD!!
VZ
PF
PF
PF
VZ
VZ
EMBER !!
HMMM
SNEASEL'S SO FAST— DO I GO WITH AIBO—
CHK
!!
BOM
—OR FAKE WITH AIBO AND USE SUDOBO ?!

LOW KICK
GG...
NOW GO!!
GOTCHA!
WHAT ?!

NKH!

TNK

DYNAMIC PUNCH!!

DGGG

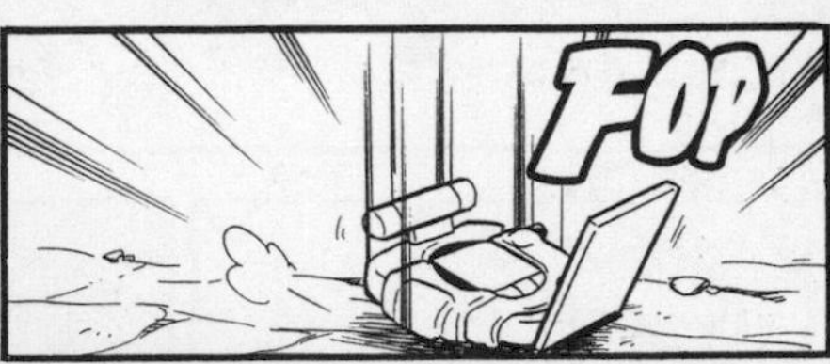

RAK RAK RAK RAK BOOM

SUDOBO—MIMIC!

URSARING—FURY SWIPES!!

RAK RAK RAK

KEEP GOING!

NEXT!

OF COURSE!

VZ

VZ

PRRRRRRT

!!

!!

...
SHF

WHAT WAS THAT?!
AND WHO ARE **YOU** ?!
CHK

SHHHH

SORRY, GOLD. BUT I HAVE TO END THIS BATTLE RIGHT NOW.
VSH!

BOM!!

HSSS

GRAAAAH
BOOM
AIBO!
H- HE'S HAD THAT ALL ALONG ?!
TYRANITAR!
TM
TM
LOOK OUT!!
TM
TM
SILVER'S NOT EVEN GIVING COM- MANDS ?!
...
KOOM
WHAT KIND OF FIGHTING IS THIS...?
HEY!
TYRANITAR'S LEVEL IS SO HIGH THAT WHEN IT GOES ON A RAMPAGE, EVEN I CAN'T CONTROL IT.
WHAT ?!

SIGH
BUT IT'S ABOUT TIME...
VP
... FOR IT TO BRING OUT...
...ITS SPECIAL ATTACK.
HOOOOO
SANDSTORM
WAAAAGH!
HSSSH
AIBO!
EXBO! SUNBO! SUDO-BO!
SHOOO

SPYUU
POLI-BO...
W-WATER GUN!
PSSSH
IT'S NO USE.
HWP
HWP
HWP
WHAT?!
RRK
FUMP
POLI-BO!
?!

...
SHHHHH

DID IT WORK ...?

... WHAT ?!

WOBBLE...

TYRANI-TAR?! IMPOS-SIBLE!!
WHAT HAP-PENED ?!
?!

TOGEPI?!
BUT WHEN...?!
POLITOED WAS A DECOY...
...SO TOGEPI COULD SLIP IN WITH DOUBLE-EDGE!

EXBO, SUNBO, SUDOBO.
AIBO, POLIBO... AND TOGEBO ...
ALL DOWN FOR THE COUNT.

FOMP
WELL, SILVER ...
...IT LOOKS LIKE I LOSE!
BUT I MADE YOU RESORT TO YOUR SIXTH POKÉMON! SO MUCH FOR YOUR HANDICAP!

HMPH ...

FSH
PAP
!
THERE YOU GO.
JAB
AND NEXT TIME... I'M GONNA WIN!!

COULD HE REALLY ...
HEY!!

...HAVE PICKED THIS UP IN THE MIDDLE OF THE SAND-STORM?

IF HE'D USED THAT TIME TO GIVE A COMMAND INSTEAD...
...THIS BATTLE COULD ACTUALLY HAVE GONE HIS WAY...
UP
LET'S GO, SNEASEL.

GOLD. YOU'VE PROVEN YOUR-SELF.
YOU SHOULD BE SATIS-FIED NOW...
...AND STOP FOLLOW-ING ME AROUND.
B-B-BON
TM

VNNN
...FOR YOUR EFFORTS, I'LL ANSWER YOUR QUESTION.
WSH
...

YOU MEAN ...?

TEAM ROCKET ATTACKED ECRUTEAK IN ORDER TO CALL FORTH HO-OH.
PAP
"CALL FORTH" ?!
IT'S SAID THAT THE TIN TOWER IS WHERE THE LEGENDARY POKÉMON HO-OH NESTS.

TEAM ROCKET HOPES THAT DESTROYING THE TIN TOWER WILL TRIGGER HO-OH'S HOMING INSTINCTS.
YOU MEAN THEY DESTROYED THE CITY... JUST TO BRING SOME POKÉMON BACK TO ITS NEST?!

AS FOR MY MISSION... IT'S TO CRUSH THEM.

AND ALSO TO FOLLOW HO-OH.
IN ORDER TO ACHIEVE THOSE ENDS...
...I CAN'T BE CHOOSY ABOUT THE MEANS.
NOT EVEN IF I HAVE TO BREAK THE LAW.

GLANCE

...
MMG...

LET'S GO!
VSH
SNEASEL. CROCO-NAW.

NOD
PLUS TOTODILE... I MEAN, CROCO-NAW... ISN'T BACK HOME YET, IS IT, EXBO?

...I STILL DON'T SEE WHY HE HAS TO FIGHT ALONE.
I DON'T CARE WHO HE'S GOING UP AGAINST ...

I'M COMING WITH YOU!!
WAIT UP!
VSH

MEAN-
WHILE,
IN
VIRIDIAN
CITY...
HM.
SHK
I
HOPE
SHE'S
DOING
WELL...
IT'S
BEEN
A WHILE
SINCE
I'VE
BEEN IN
KANTO
...
DINGDONG

AND DIDN'T I GIVE YOU... DODUO?

WOOM

FISHERMAN!

I HEAR YOU WENT THROUGH A LOT LAST YEAR, HUH?!
HA HA.

IT'S SO GOOD TO SEE YOU!!
WAHAHAHA! I'VE MISSED YOU, YELLOW!

AND PEOPLE SEEM A LOT MORE RELAXED LATELY.

HOW'VE THINGS BEEN SINCE THEN?
IT'S BEEN OKAY. THE CITIES OF KANTO ARE MOSTLY REBUILT...

HUH?! WHO'S THIS ONE?!

POING
CHUCHU, MY PIKACHU.

I FOUND CHUCHU INJURED IN THE VIRIDIAN FOREST AND BROUGHT IT BACK WITH ME.

LOOKS LIKE CHUCHU'S REALLY TAKEN TO YOU!

SO, FISHER-MAN, WHAT BRINGS YOU HERE?

I'VE MISSED YOU!
AND... WELL. I HAVE A FAVOR TO ASK.
A FAVOR?

YEAH. CAN YOU COME TO JOHTO WITH ME?
WHY JOHTO?

FWOOOOO
I LOOKED INTO WHAT YOU ASKED ME ABOUT BEFORE...
THE BIG FLYING-TYPE POKÉMON THAT DISAPPEARED A YEAR AGO IN JOHTO.

THE THING'S DANGEROUS. I CAN'T HANDLE IT MYSELF.
I NEED A SKILLED TRAINER.

IN THAT CASE, I'M HARDLY THE ONE TO ASK!
THE ONLY REASON I WAS ABLE TO WIN A YEAR AGO WAS BECAUSE OF EVERYONE ELSE'S HELP!
BUT... WHO ELSE CAN I TURN TO?
...
HM

HOW ABOUT RED?
THAT RED?
HOW MANY REDS DO YOU KNOW?
VOOP

GO, VENU-SAUR !!

FSH

VINE WHIP !!

WHIP

ONLY SOMETIMES... BUT...

... WHEN THEY DO, THEY GO TOTALLY NUMB.

MY ANKLES TOO... WHERE LORELEI'S ICE RINGS GOT ME.

GRIP...

LAKE OF RAGE
...

BEGIN MOBILI-ZATION.
CHK

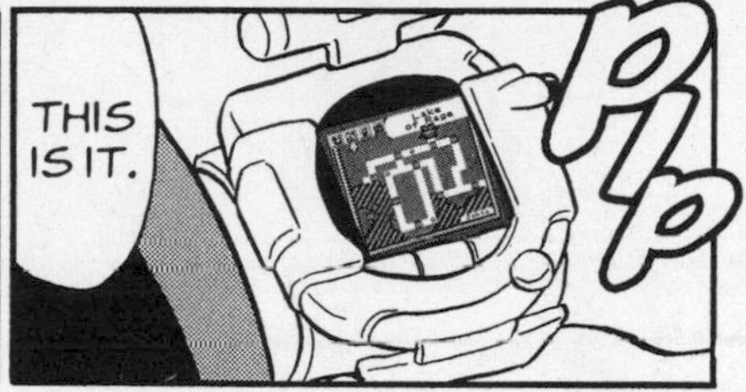
PIP
THIS IS IT.

WEIRD, I KNOW I SAW HIM AROUND HERE...
HFF
BUT WHERE'D HE GO ?!

LET'S... REST AWHILE ...
HOO
HFF HF

PLIP...
HUH ...?

ZWOOSH

EEYOW!!

112 Raise the Red Gyarados

SILVER !!

VZ
AAAAAA
HUH ?

TM
GOTCHA!! LET'S GO, EXBO!!

OKAY.
CHK

VSH

WP
WHOA.
WHAT'S THIS THING YOU HAVE ABOUT GOING IT ALONE?!
I CAN HELP!

BOOM
SHOVE
WAGH ?!
HEY!
IF YOU KNOW WHAT'S GOING ON IN THIS...
IF YOU WANT TO FOLLOW, TAKE A LOOK AROUND YOU.
HUH ?
PLASH
SENSE ?
CAN'T YOU SENSE IT?
POP
?
WHAT'S GOING ON?!
D
ZZZ

ELECTRO-MAGNETIC WAVES FILLING THE AIR...
KVVZZZT
... AND FORCING POKÉMON EVOLUTIONS. HENCE THE MASS GYARADOS OUTBREAK.

FORC-ING ...?!
BUT WHERE ARE THE WAVES COMING FROM?!
VWAH
GET BACK HERE!

YOU KEEP THEM CONFINED THERE!
YOU'RE NOT THE BOSS OF ME!!

DOOM
YAAA!

PAPA PAPAP
SHOOT!
POLIBO! DOUBLE-SLAP!!

PAPAPAPAP
PLOSH
PLISH
THERE'S NO END IN SIGHT.
MWK
POP
MORE?!

HOW DID I LET MYSELF GET STUCK WITH THIS?!
IDIOT!!

...
PLISH
PLASH

CAN'T WASTE MY RESOURCES FIGHTING ALL OF THEM. GOT TO HIT THE SOURCE.
BUT WHERE'S THE TRANS-MITTER?

PLOOSH
THERE'S NO WAY TO STOP 'EM!!
YAAAAA!!
THE TOWN'S GONNA BE HELPLESS!!
IT'S GOT TO BE NEAR HERE... BUT I DON'T SEE ANYTHING MAN-MADE!
WE GOTTA STOP THE WAVES!
BUT WHERE ARE THEY COMING FROM?!
WHAT IS THE TRANS-MITTER?!

ELM RESIDENCE

I DON'T LIKE THIS...
WHAT'S UP, PROFESSOR?

CAN YOU GET IN TOUCH WITH GOLD RIGHT NOW?
OH... ACTUALLY...

THE CONNECTION'S DOWN.
KXXZ
NOTHING BUT STATIC.
ZXXZZZ

IS IT BROKEN?
NOT BROKEN. SOME SORT OF ELECTROMAGNETIC INTERFERENCE.

I JUST HOPE GOLD ISN'T CAUGHT UP IN ANYTHING DANGEROUS...

!
DZZZZ
ZZZZT
A RED... GYARA-DOS... ?!
IT'S ACTING WEIRD TOO!
!
?!
COULD IT BE ...?
THE WAVE IS STRON-GER?!

THE TRANSMITTER IS...THIS POKÉMON?!

CAN'T REACH IT FROM HERE! YOU GOTTA CAPTURE IT!
HWOO
I'VE JUST GOTTA STOP IT! WHIRL-POOL!!
POKÉ-BALL!
OKAY! PURSUIT!
YES !!
!
BOOM

...
THEY'RE ALL GOING BACK TO THE LAKE.
PLOOSH
PLSH
PIPIPI
I GUESS WE ACTUALLY PULLED IT OFF...

WHAT'RE YOU DOING?
ANA-LYZING THE WAVE'S FRE-QUENCY.
SO I CAN TRACK DOWN THE ULTI-MATE SOURCE... AND DESTROY IT!
PIP
GOOD THINK-ING!

BUT WHY WOULD ANYBODY DO THIS...
ARTIFI-CIALLY FORCING POKÉMON TO EVOLVE?
SHHHHH

IS IT LIKE THE EARTH-QUAKE ...?
HMPH

...

GOLD, THIS IS MY LAST WARNING.

DON'T GET INVOLVED WITH ME.

THE OPPONENT I'M PURSUING NOW IS FAR STRONGER THAN THOSE TEAM ROCKET STOOGES WE FOUGHT IN ECRUTEAK.

AN AMATEUR TRAINER LIKE YOU CAN ONLY GET IN MY WAY.

I'M ALREADY IN-VOLVED!

WHAT?

...THAT I PICK MY OWN BATTLES !!
IT'S ABOUT TIME YOU LEARNED, SILVER...
SSSSS
!
! IT CAN'T BE!
I'VE SEEN THIS FOG... SOME-WHERE ...
HUH ?!
FOG ?!
HA HA HA HA HA!
HA HA HA!
THAT GUY!!

LOOK WHO'S TALKING!
I THOUGHT YOU STAYED IN YOUR FOREST!

YOU TWO AGAIN ...
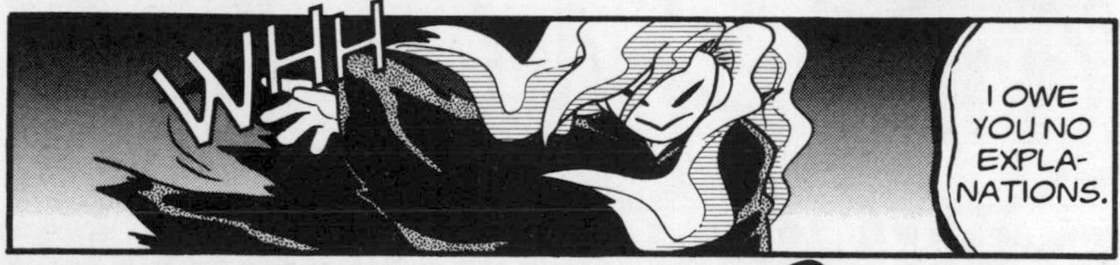
I OWE YOU NO EXPLANATIONS.
WHH

YOU'RE RIGHT! LET'S JUST SETTLE THIS FIGHT!
GOLD! STOP MOVING AROUND OR YOU'LL PLAY RIGHT INTO HIS HANDS!

SSS...
...

WHAT AM I SUPPOSED TO DO, STAND STILL?!

DYNAMIC PUNCH!
CHOK
113 Delibird Delivery – 1
YES! IT CONNECTED!!
WE REALLY ARE STRONGER!!
TING
YOUR HAND'S FROZEN?!
HUH?
SH
THIS TIME I'M NOT GONNA...

VSH
SHOOT...
YOU'LL REGRET THAT!!
MMG
WOOOO
HAHAHA... THAT'S WHAT YOU CALL STRONGER?
!
KINGDRA!
TM
WMP
!
HWAH
TWISTER!!
BUTT OUTTA THIS!
I OWE THIS CREEP BIG-TIME AND I'M GONNA–
SHUT UP! LOOK AROUND YOU!

!
ICE THORNS?! BUT HOW-?!
...
GULP
IF YOU'D CHARGED, YOU'D BE HASH NOW.
OH, I GET IT... HIDDEN BY THE FOG.
...!
PRO-FESSOR ELM?!
PRRRRT
PEEP
Professor Elm
GOLD, IS THAT YOU?!
I'M SO GLAD I CAUGHT YOU!

I'VE COMPLETED MY ANALYSIS OF THAT GOLD POWDER.
I ALMOST CAN'T BRING MYSELF TO BELIEVE IT...

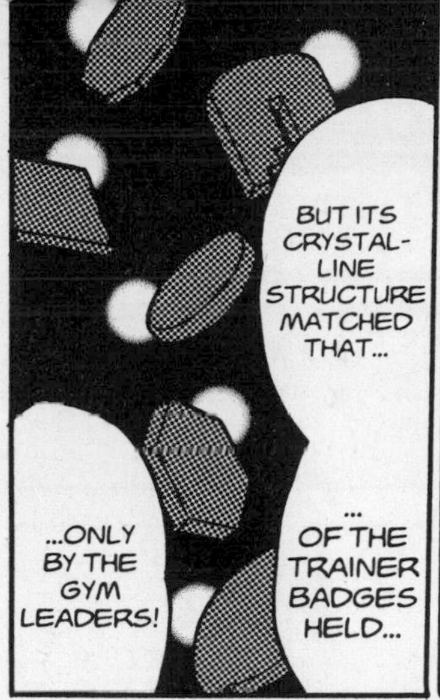
BUT ITS CRYSTAL-LINE STRUCTURE MATCHED THAT...
...OF THE TRAINER BADGES HELD...
...ONLY BY THE GYM LEADERS!

THE MASKED MAN YOU FOUGHT IN ILEX FOREST MAY BE A FORMER GYM LEADER! BUT WE DON'T KNOW WHICH ONE!
IT'S HARD TO IMAGINE A MORE DANGEROUS OPPONENT THAN A GYM LEADER!

BUT KNOWING YOU, YOU'LL RUSH RIGHT INTO COMBAT WITH HIM!
NO MATTER WHAT... DON'T FIGHT HIM!

DO YOU UNDER-STAND, GOLD?
PIP!
BZZ BZZ
...

THANKS FOR THE WARNING, PROFES-SOR...
HMF

I'M TIRED OF YOU PESTS ...

S...

... BUZZING ME!

BLIZZARD !!

HOO...

!!

TINK
TINK
THE TREES ARE FREEZING OVER?!
NOW I SEE HOW HE MADE THE SPIKES!

WHICH ONE SHALL I TAKE CARE OF FIRST?
OR SHOULD I GET RID OF BOTH OF YOU AT ONCE?

YOU CAN'T RUN AWAY LIKE LAST TIME ...
!!
... SILVER.
JAB
HSH
SNEASEL !!

SILVER?!
WHAT'S GOING ON?!
WAFT
DELI-BIRD!!
SHHOOOO
ICY WIND!!

VRR
WKWKWK
THAT'S THE TARGET!
!!
GAH!
WHAT ...?!
SILVER !!
UGH!
WOK
FOOLED YOU!
WD D
NN...
FMP

THEY... KNOW EACH OTHER ...?
NNG...

IT'S BEEN FIVE YEARS, SILVER.
HOW PERFECT THAT YOU'D BE THE ONE FOLLOWING ME.

PER-HAPS ...

WHAT ARE YOU THINKING OF?
RE-VENGE ?
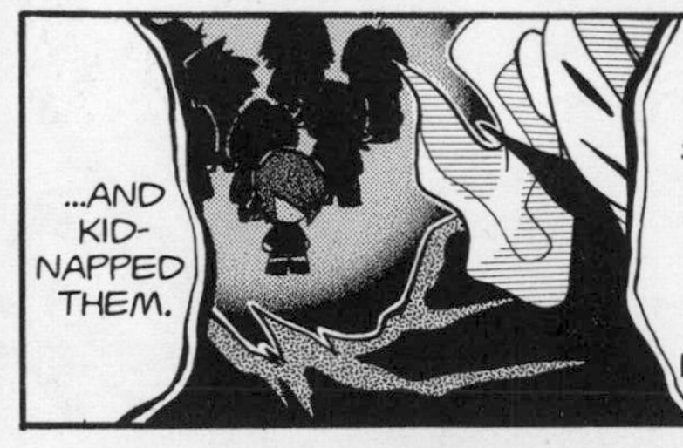
...AND KID-NAPPED THEM.

HEY, HEY! WHAT'S ALL THIS ABOUT?
NINE YEARS AGO, I SEARCHED THE LAND FOR CHILDREN WITH HIGH TRAINER POTENTIAL ...

YOU WERE KIDNAPPING KIDS?! FOR WHAT?!
WHAT ELSE? TO USE AS MY SLAVES.

WHY WAS THE ONCE POWERFUL TEAM ROCKET DE-STROYED?
BECAUSE OF DISSENSION WITHIN ITS RANKS.
POWER REQUIRES OBEDIENCE! SERVANTS AS UN-THINKING AS THOSE GYARADOS!

WOO
CHILDREN CAN BE MOLDED INTO PERFECT SLAVES IF YOU TEACH THEM EARLY ENOUGH.
JUST LIKE A GYARA-DOS, TRAINED FROM WHEN IT'S A MAGI-KARP.
WAHA-HAHA HAHA-HA!

KRRG
YOU... ARE GONNA PAY...

!
CHK

GLINT
DON'T DO ANY-THING RASH, SILVER!

HMF

NOT UNLESS YOU WANT SOMETHING TO HAPPEN TO HIM.

HEHEHEH... AS I THOUGHT.
YOU'VE GONE WEAK, SILVER.
IF YOU'D STAYED UNDER ME...
YOU'D HAVE BECOME THE PERFECT TRAINER, FREE OF ALL WEAKNESSES... INCLUDING COMPASSION.
NNG...

YOU'RE WRONG!!
WHAT?

YOU THINK SILVER'S WEAK?
THEN YOU DON'T KNOW WHAT STRENGTH IS!
OH?

I'VE SEEN HIS STRENGTH OVER AND OVER AGAIN!

AND IT'S A STRENGTH THAT GOES DEEP IN HIS SOUL!

EXACTLY THE STRENGTH A GREAT TRAINER NEEDS!

...

YOU'RE THE WEAK ONE... LEANING ON THOSE TEAM ROCKET MORONS!

YOU'RE A MOUTHY LITTLE ...

YOU'RE SMARTER THAN I THOUGHT.

I'M FINALLY PUTTING SOME PIECES TOGETHER!

LIKE HOW THIS CHUMP IS PULLING ALL THE STRINGS...

...AND HOW I'M GONNA HELP YOU BEAT HIM!

!

SAVE THE ARGU-MENTS.

...WHAT-EVER.

THIS GUY USES POKÉMON AND PEOPLE LIKE THINGS!

HE'S A DISGRACE TO EVERY TRAINER!!

LET'S SHUT HIM DOWN!!

EXBO!
SNEASEL!
HE-HEHEH...
I WARNED YOU AGAINST THIS...
...BUT I'M GLAD YOU DIDN'T LISTEN!
VWAH
!!
ZSH

114 Delibird Delivery – 2
FLAME WHEEL! ICY WIND!
A DARING COMBINATION. TOO BAD...
HEH
YEAH?
TP
HMM...
INTER-ESTING.
TP

SHK
HEY!
WK
...! THEY DISAP-PEARED?!
PF
...IT CAN'T LAST.
PF
WK
UNGH!
I'M GONNA—

KINNNG

VSH

QUICK ATTACK !!

DG DG DG DG

ROCK SMASH !!

OUT OF MY WAY, GOLD!!
WOM
NGH!
HEY!! WHAT—? ICE?!
TINK
FWAH

WSH
STOP!!
HEH. SO FEARLESS.
TM
VM
YOU'RE FILLED WITH SO MUCH COURAGE...
MURKROW!! KNOCK THEM DOWN!!
AFTER ALL THIS TIME, STILL SO NAIVE...
I KNEW EXACTLY WHAT YOU WERE DOING.
VK VK VK VK
VP VP VP
...THAT YOU'D FALL FOR A TRICK LIKE THAT!
VK
...YOU'VE GOT NO ROOM FOR BRAINS!

WAM
YOU WANTED TO SEPARATE ME FROM GOLD.
!
PEK
PEK
PEK
BUT AGAINST YOUR WICKEDNESS...
VWOP
...I'LL FIGHT ANYTIME... ANYWHERE.
INCLUDING THE MIDDLE OF THIS LAKE...
...WHERE I JUST LED YOU !!
CHK

!
THE GYARA-DOS— THAT I EVOLVED!!
LOOKS LIKE I LEARNED SOME-THING FROM YOU AFTER ALL.
SNEER
AGH!!

YOU ...
I CAUGHT THE ONE YOU WERE USING AS A TRANS-MITTER.
THAT MEANS THEY'VE ALL BEEN FREED FROM YOUR CONTROL...
AND THEY'RE ANGRY!! HYPER BEAM!!
FSH

OKAY! THAT MELTED THE ICE ON MY SHOES—BUT WE GOTTA DO SOME-THING ABOUT THESE TWO!
GRRR
NOW—
ZIP
ZIP
ZIP
AIBO, DO YOUR STUFF!
GONK
DOUBLE TEAM!!
WHERE ARE YOU?!
VZ
SILVER !!
WE DID IT, AIBO!

!

HUH?! THE LAKE'S FROZEN ?!

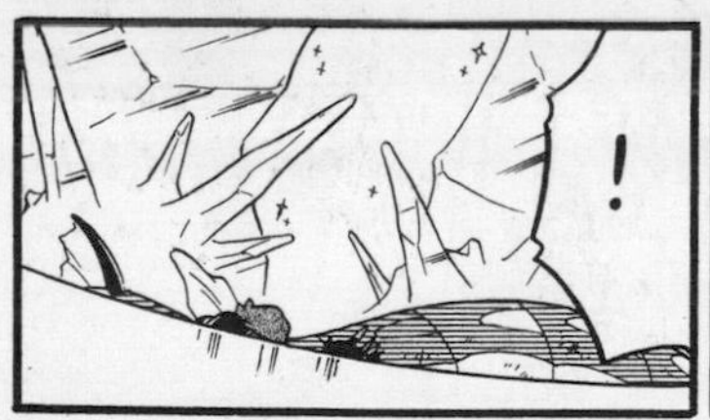

!!
CHOOM
WHERE ARE YOU?!
SILVER !!
DM
YOUR TURN !!
DM
DM
DM
DM
DM
IF YOU'VE HURT HIM—!
AIBO !!
ZNK
NG
ZK
ZK
ZK

YOU...
HEH HEH. QUITE A LETDOWN AFTER ALL YOUR TALK.

HEH
NOT EVEN AS GOOD AS MY OLD SLAVE.

YOU DIDN'T HAVE TO DO THAT!
YOU'D ALREADY WON THAT BATTLE.
GRP
YOU... SCUM...

BE-SIDES...
BUT LIFE WILL BE SIMPLER WITHOUT HIM.
WAFT
PER-HAPS NOT.

"DESERVES" ?!
WHO ARE **YOU** TO SAY WHAT ANYBODY DESERVES ?!

HE RAN AWAY FROM ME.
FOR THAT, HE DESERVES TO BE PUNISHED.

SHH

WHAT ...?!
...!!
DOOOM
YAAA-AAA!

CHU!
PIKA!

HUH?
TPTPTP
CHU!

HEY, RED.
YO! YELLOW! LONG TIME NO SEE!

YOU FEEL-ING SHY?
PAT PAT
WHAT'S THIS, PIKA?
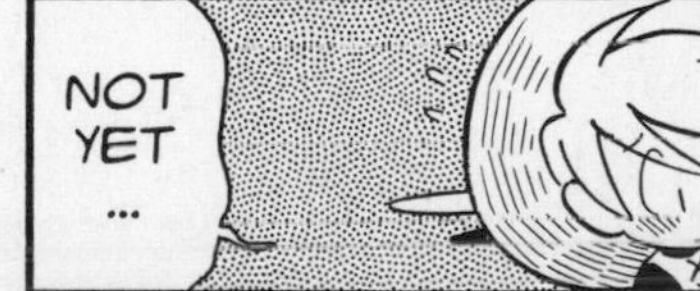
NOT YET ...

PSS PSS
HAVE YOU TOLD HIM ABOUT WHAT'S IN YOUR HAT?

IT'S NOTH-ING.
SERIOUS-LY! DON'T WORRY!

UM... RED? WHAT HAP-PENED WITH YOUR HAND ...?
OH. YOU SAW?
JUST THE GHOST OF AN OLD INJURY.

115 Forretress of Solitude

THE POKÉMON ASSOCIATION KNOWS YOU INSIDE OUT.
THIS'LL BE A PIECE O' CAKE IF THERE EVER WAS ONE.
HONESTLY, RED, I THINK YOU CAN EASE OFF.
RED

YOU KNOW SOMETHING I DON'T?
I'VE JUST GOT FAITH IN YOU, IS ALL!
DINGDONG
MORE VISITORS?

YEAH ...?
KRIII
HOW YOU DOIN', RED?
MISTY! BROCK!
HERE'S THE VIDEO I PROMISED OF MY GYM LEADER EXAM! PLUS NOTES!
AND HERE'S MINE!

THANK YOU! THESE'LL HELP A TON!!
TO-MORROW, HUH? FINALLY!
DO YOU HAVE A PLAN OF ATTACK?

YOU'RE A SHOO-IN NO MATTER WHAT.
GOOD LUCK ANY-HOW!

GUTS & WILL!
... VERY FUNNY.

Charizard.
I CAN'T HELP BEING NERVOUS ...

MY POKÉ-MON ARE READY ...
AND I'VE MEMO-RIZED EVERY ATTACK.
IT'D BE A SURE THING ...

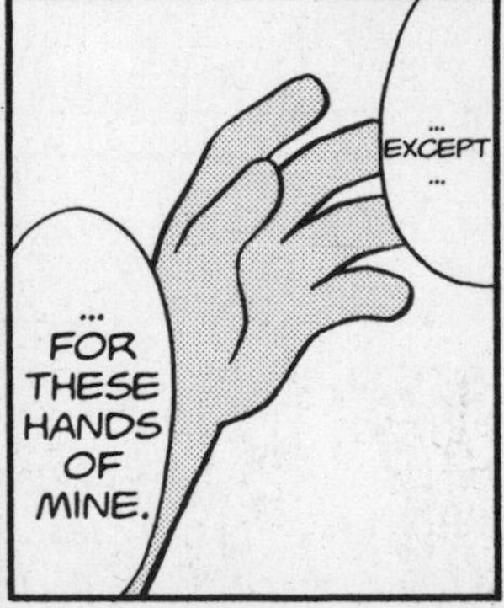
... EXCEPT ...
... FOR THESE HANDS OF MINE.

I NEED A PLAN OF ATTACK.
BUT ALSO... A BACKUP PLAN IF I GO NUMB DURING THE FIGHT.

VIRIDIAN
GYM
DAY OF BATTLE

I SHALL READ THE RULES OF THE EXAM.

THE CANDIDATE MUST DEFEAT SIX POKÉMON. THOSE POKÉMON WILL HAVE NO TRAINERS.
YADA

YADA
YADA

THEY WILL BATTLE ON THEIR OWN INITIATIVE.

THE CANDIDATE IS ALLOWED SIX POKÉMON OF HIS OWN. BUT...

...IF EVEN ONE OF THEM IS INCAPACITATED, THE CANDIDATE IS DISQUALIFIED.
B-BOM
BOMB
OM

PLACE YOUR POKÉMON IN THE POKÉ BALLS, PLEASE.

...
GG

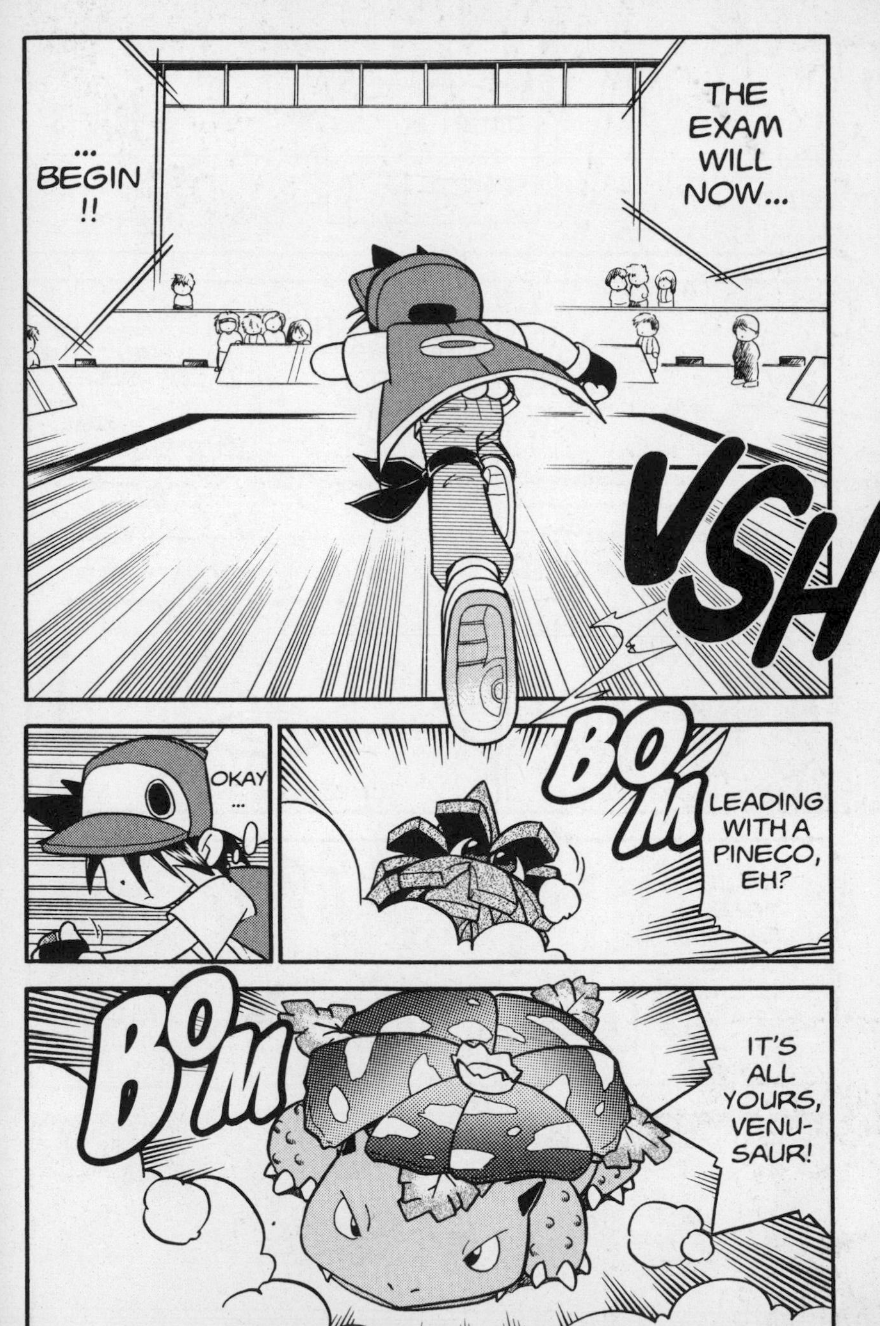

THE EXAM WILL NOW...
...BEGIN!!
VSH
BOOM
OKAY...
LEADING WITH A PINECO, EH?
BOOM
IT'S ALL YOURS, VENUSAUR!

BOM
NOW A FORRE-TRESS!
WHPP
VINE WHIP!
WHPP
AGAIN !!
OOO
OR... MAKE THAT THREE...
HE'S ALREADY THROUGH TWO!!
HERE COMES NUMBER FOUR.
KEEP UP THE PACE!
GOMP

ANOTHER FORRETRESS—AND IT'S UNLEASHED SPIKES!!

BOM

SHM

SHM

!!

SHM

SNOR! BELLY DRUM!!

NOW RETURN!

BOM

FUAAA

SAUR—SWEET SCENT!

BM

YELLOW! DOESN'T BELLY DRUM TURN PHYSICAL STRENGTH INTO ATTACK STRENGTH? SO...

VOP VIP

BOM

NOW IT'S AZU-MARILL... WITH ITS WHIRL-POOL!!

WOOO

WOOO

SHOOT... CAN'T SWAP OUT WHILE I'M CAUGHT IN THIS!

MEGA KICK!!
SO QUICK!!
GOOD JOB, SNOR!!
FAP
BON
RETURN!!
OKAY, VEE... IT'S DOWN TO YOU!
BOM
BOM
FINAL OPPONENT... PORYGON2!
SNAP
?!

AND HERE COMES THE ZAP CANNON!

THEY'VE LOCKED ON!

GLEEM
STORE POWER—
WITH MORNING SUN!!
NOW—
ZING
PSYCHIC!
FINISH IT!!
PORY-GON2 IS DOWN!!
PHEW
THE EXAM'S OVER!
GRIP
...
BRRR

I'LL EVEN TAKE THE EXAM... IF YOU INSIST.

YOU'RE BACK?!

BLUE ?!

BLUE !!

TM TM TM

WHO ARE YOU?!

ARGH!

THROB

GRAB

...

※ SEE POKÉMON ADVENTURES VOLUME 7

HEY! HEY! WAIT JUST ONE MINUTE!

WHO DO YOU THINK YOU ARE?!

STROLLING IN HERE TALKING ABOUT TAKING OVER THIS GYM?!

A GYM LEADER HAS TO PROVE THAT HE...

DOMM

!

116 Rock, Paper... Scizor

D-D...DM
WHAT WAS THAT?!
EARTH-QUAKE!!

HEY! YOU!!
VM

!!

EVERY-ONE, REMAIN CALM!!
CALM !!

STOP RED! HE'S IN NO CONDI-TION TO FIGHT!
VM
O-OKAY!

DDM..M

!
WILD POKÉ-MON?!
BUT WHY ?!
HERE THEY COME!
NO TIME TO EVACUATE THE GYM! RED–PROTECT THE ENTRANCE!!
GOT IT!
RRAR
POOM
SCIZOR! METAL CLAW!!
KIIIN

GO!
WOK
FAST—
AS
USUAL
!!
!
OOCH
OKAY,
THEN!
HMF
EXEGGUTOR'S
OLD TRICK—
INTIMIDATING
THE ENEMY
WITH ITS THREE
HEADS!!
RED,
ARE
YOU
...?!
I'M
OKAY!
STAY
BACK,
YELLOW!!
WSH

EEP

VWM

EXEGGUTOR'S AFRAID! BUT OF WHAT?!

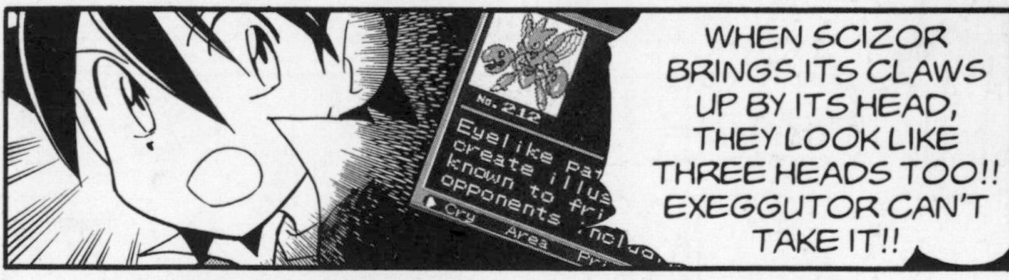

WOK
FALSE SWIPE!
THWAP
GOOD!
BON
YEAH !!
B-B-BON

LIKE NO ONE BUT PROFESSOR OAK'S GRANDSON COULD!!

YOU DID IT, BLUE!!

UM... NOT TO MENTION ...

THE PRO-FESSOR'S... GRAND-SON?!

IT'S TH-TH-THE COMMITTEE CAR. IS SOME-THING...?
THAT WAS THE "POKÉMON MARCH."
WHOSE CAR IS THIS?

YOUR STUPID SONG COULDA KILLED US!
I-I'M SO SORRY... I...I DIDN'T REALIZE...
YOU FOOL! WILD POKÉMON LOVE THAT SONG! NO WONDER THEY WERE SWARMING!

BUT IF YOU WANT PEOPLE TO KEEP TRUSTING YOU...
YOU'D BETTER FIND SOMEBODY AS GOOD AS RED. AND QUICK.
IF YOU DECIDE I'M NOT QUALIFIED, FINE.
WHAT?! WHAT?! WHAT?!
MR. DIREC-TOR.

Y...YOU THINK...?

I FOUND THAT INFO YOU WERE LOOKING FOR.
!

FWA
RED!

BLUE ...

ASK MY SISTER FOR MORE DETAILS.

MAKE THE ANNOUNCEMENT! WE HAVE FOUND A NEW LEADER FOR THE VIRIDIAN CITY GYM!
WHAT?! BUT WHAT ABOUT THE COMMITTEE'S APPROVAL?! AND THE EXAM?!

IT'LL BE FINE.
HE ALREADY FIXED ONE OF OUR MISTAKES.
LET'S NOT ADD ANOTHER ONE.

WHAT WILL AN EXAM SHOW? WE KNOW HE HAS SKILL, LEADERSHIP ABILITY ...
...AND MOST IMPORTANT OF ALL... PLENTY OF LOCAL RESPECT!
GO!
B-BUT...

TUG
OKAY.
RED?
RED!
RED
I FINALLY HAVE THE INFO I NEEDED...
...ON HOW TO HEAL MYSELF!
YOU'RE HEADING OUT ALREADY?
YEAH. I CAN'T WAIT.
YOU MEAN... HIS HANDS AND FEET CAN BE FIXED?!
SOUNDS LIKE IT!

THERE'S THIS SECRET HOT SPRING ON MT. SILVER...
...WHERE POKÉMON GO TO HEAL THEIR WOUNDS.
SEEMS SABRINA'S UP THERE. SIMILAR SYMPTOMS ...
... AFTER SUFFERING THE SAME ATTACK.
I CAN'T BELIEVE IT! AFTER A WHOLE YEAR OF TRYING TO GET WELL!
EX-CEPT ...
?
THERE ARE A LOT OF POWERFUL POKÉMON ON THAT MOUNTAIN.
TO GET THIS CURE... HE'S REALLY GOING TO HAVE TO WANT IT.
OKAY, CHARIZARD! LET'S GO!
BOM

PIKA, YOU WAIT FOR ME AT YELLOW AND CHUCHU'S PLACE.
!
LOOK AFTER PIKA, YELLOW!
YOU'RE SURE ...?
SORRY, PIKA. I DON'T WANT TO BE BLAMING MYSELF FOR ANYTHING HAPPENING TO YOU.
GUIDE HIM SAFELY, CHARI-ZARD.
WE'RE OFF—TO MT. SILVER!!
...

WATCH OUT FOR POKÉMON ADVENTURES VOLUME 10!

NEXT VOLUME PREVIEW!
YELLOW TRAVELS TO JOHTO! GOLD AND SILVER VANISH AT THE LAKE! AND SOMEONE ELSE IS ABOUT TO JOIN THE STORY...THE BEARER OF THE THIRD POKÉDEX!
THE BEST TEAM!
POKÉMON ADVENTURES 10!
WITH THE BEST GEAR !!
HWOO
BUT WHO IS THE SHADOW ?!
Here comes
...THE CATCHER!!!
ON SALE NOW
Hidenori Kusaka
Satoshi Yamamoto

ADVENTURE ROUTE MAP 9

FROM ILEX FOREST TO MAHOGANY AND THE LAKE OF RAGE! (WITH A LOOK AT THE VETERAN TRAINERS' MOVEMENTS TOO!)

"GOTTA CATCH 'EM ALL!!"

ADVENTURE ROUTE MAP 9

SILVER'S SECRETS!
POKÉDEX
152 CHIKORITA
153 -------------
154 -------------
155 CYNDAQUIL
156 QUILAVA
157 -------------
▶158 TOTODILE
159 CROCONAW
160 -------------
MAIN CHARACTER: SILVER
BADGES: 4
POKÉDEX : 10 POKÉMON
NUMBER SEEN
54
NUMBER CAUGHT
10
Silver is always seeking Pokémon who'll help him fulfill his objective!
The Team Thus Far:
Seems to favor Dark-types. An attack-oriented team.
TEAM SILVER

SNEASEL: LV 36
TYPE 1 / DARK
TYPE 2 / ICE
TRAINER / SILVER
NO.215

THE TEAM LEADER! BEATS OPPONENTS WITH SHARP CLAWS, SHARP WITS AND FAST MOVES!

MURKROW: LV 29
TYPE 1 / DARK
TYPE 2 / FLYING
TRAINER / SILVER
NO.198

LOOKS LIKE THE WINGS OF DARKNESS AS IT CARRIES SILVER—AND GIVES HIM A BIG ADVANTAGE IN NIGHT BATTLES!

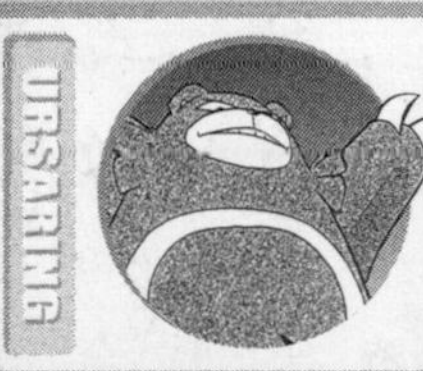

URSARING: LV 35
TYPE 1 / NORMAL
TRAINER / SILVER
NO.217

THE HEAVIEST MEMBER OF THE TEAM, CAUGHT USING A HEAVY BALL—AND A HEAVY-DUTY FIGHTER!

CROCONAW: LV 29
TYPE 1 / WATER
TRAINER / SILVER
NO.159

KINGDRA: LV 33
TYPE 1 / WATER
TYPE 2 / DRAGON
TRAINER / SILVER
NO.230

GYARADOS: LV 30
TYPE 1 / WATER
TYPE 2 / FLYING
TRAINER / SILVER
NO.130

Croconaw evolved from the Totodile that Silver stole from Professor Elm's lab. Kingdra evolved during a trade with Gold. A rare red Gyarados appears. Why does he want three Water-types? And who did he borrow Tyranitar from? There's a hint in the Poké Ball it came out of…

TYRANITAR NO. 248

Message from
Hidenori Kusaka

For me the 21st century began when I got my first Game Boy Advance… a Pokémon Center limited edition! I was totally excited! Suicune blue! (Of course, I get excited easily.) I still play it to get in the right creative mood…

Message from
MATO

Gold, Silver, Red, Blue, Yellow and all those Pokémon… The four years I've spent with them have seemed long, but it also feels like just yesterday that we first met. It's an amazing feeling. We've been able to have this great run because of the enthusiasm of you, our fans. And so, with deep gratitude, we bring you this book!

More Adventures Coming Soon...

The journey continues! In order to assist Professor Oak's research, a young Trainer, Crystal, hits the streets with a new Pokédex in hand! Her goal is to capture all kinds of wild Pokémon! And what will happen now that the Legendary Pokémon Suicune has awakened?!

AVAILABLE NOW!

Pokémon MOVIE

Legend tells of The Sea Temple, which contains a treasure with the power to take over the world. But its location remains hidden and requires a mysterious key. Can Ash, Pikachu and their friends prevent the unveiling of these powerful secrets?

Pokémon Ranger and the Temple of the Sea

Own it on DVD today!

Pokémon USA, Inc.

www.pokemon.com

www.viz.com

© 2006 Pokémon. © 1997-2006 Nintendo, Creatures, GAME FREAK, TV Tokyo, ShoPro, JR Kikaku. © Pikachu Project 2005. Pokémon properties are trademarks of Nintendo.

What's Better Than Catching Pokémon? Becoming one!

Pokémon Mystery Dungeon
GINJI'S RESCUE TEAM

Ginji is a normal boy until the day he turns into a Torchic and joins Mudkip's Rescue Team. Now he must help any and all Pokémon in need...but will Ginji be able to rescue his human self?

Become part of the adventure—and mystery—with *Pokémon Mystery Dungeon: Ginji's Rescue Team.* Buy yours today!

www.pokemon.com

vizkids
Pokémon Mystery Dungeon
GINJI'S RESCUE TEAM
Inspired by the brand-new Nintendo games
RED RESCUE TEAM
BLUE RESCUE TEAM
Story and art by
Makoto Mizobuchi

www.viz.com vizkids

© 2006 Pokémon. © 1995-2006 Nintendo/Creatures Inc./GAME FREAK inc.
© 1993-2006 CHUNSOFT. TM & ® are trademarks of Nintendo.
© 2006 Makoto MIZOBUCHI/Shogakukan Inc.

Pokémon™
BLACK AND WHITE

MEET POKÉMON TRAINERS BLACK AND WHITE

THE WAIT IS FINALLY OVER! Meet Pokémon Trainer Black! His entire life, Black has dreamed of winning the Pokémon League... Now Black embarks on a journey to explore the Unova region and fill a Pokédex for Professor Juniper. Time for Black's first Pokémon Trainer Battle ever!

Who will Black choose as his next Pokémon? Who would *you* choose?

Plus, meet Pokémon Snivy, Tepig, Oshawott and many more new Pokémon of the unexplored Unova region!

Story by HIDENORI KUSAKA

Art by SATOSHI YAMAMOTO

$4.99 USA | $6.99 CAN

Inspired by the hit video games *Pokémon Black Version* and *Pokémon White Version!*

Available Now at your local bookstore or comic store

© 2011 Pokémon.
©1995-2011 Nintendo/Creatures Inc./GAME FREAK inc.
Pokémon properties are trademarks of Nintendo.
POCKET MONSTER SPECIAL © 1997 Hidenori KUSAKA, Satoshi YAMAMOTO/Shogakukan

vizkids www.vizkids.com

HEROES OF MANGA viz media 25 YEARS www.viz.com/25years

Take a trip with Pokémon

ALL THAT PIKACHU!

ANI-MANGA™

Meet Pikachu and all-star Pokémon! Two complete Pikachu stories taken from the Pokémon movies—all in a full color manga.

Buy yours today!

POKéMON

www.pokemon.com

© 2007 Pokémon. © 1997-2007 Nintendo, Creatures, GAME FREAK, TV Tokyo, ShoPro, JR Kikaku.
© PIKACHU PROJECT 1998.
Pokémon properties are trademarks of Nintendo.
Cover art subject to change.

vizkids

www.viz.c

This way!

THIS IS THE END OF THIS GRAPHIC NOVEL!

To properly enjoy this VIZ Media graphic novel, please turn it around and begin reading from right to left.

This book has been printed in the original Japanese format in order to preserve the orientation of the original artwork. Have fun with it!

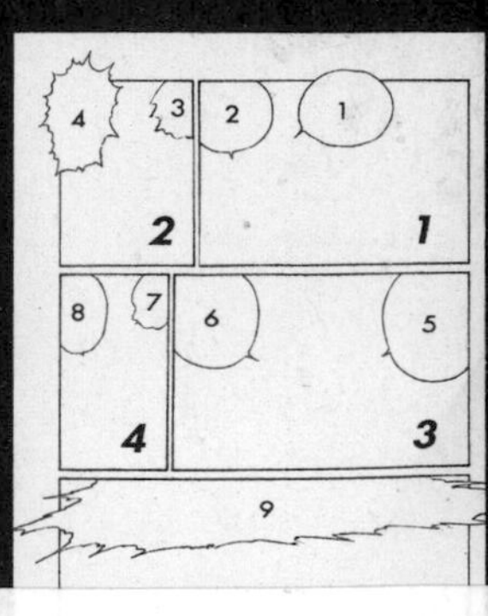

CALGARY PUBLIC LIBRARY
DECEMBER 2013